FLOATING CLOUDS, FLOATING DREAMS

FLOATING CLOUDS, FLOATING DREAMS

FAVORITE ASIAN FOLKTALES

Edited by
I. K. JUNNE

F
J
8222

DOUBLEDAY & COMPANY, INC.
GARDEN CITY, NEW YORK

ISBN: 0-385-05204-9 Trade
      0-385-05358-4 Prebound
Library of Congress Catalog Card Number 73–15349
Copright © 1974 by I. K. Junne
Printed in the United States of America
First Edition

Grateful acknowledgment is made to the following for permission to reprint their material:

"The Magic Listening Cap" and "The Rice Cake That Rolled Away" from *The Magic Listening Cap,* copyright © 1955, by Yoshiko Uchida. Reprinted by permission of Harcourt, Brace & World, Inc.

"The Treasure of Li-Po" and "The Fox's Daughter" from *The Treasure of Li-Po* by Alice Ritchie, copyright © 1949, by Harcourt, Brace & World, Inc. and reprinted with their permission and with the permission of Mrs. M. T. Parson and The Hogarth Press.

"Prince Ahmed and the Fairy Peribanou," "The Adventures of Little Peachling" and "Hok Lee and the Dwarfs" from *Fairy Tales of the Orient,* copyright © 1965, by Pearl S. Buck and Lyle Kenyon Engel. Reprinted by permission of Simon & Schuster, Inc.

"Greedy and Speedy," "The Hermit and the Mouse" and "The Monkey Gardeners" from *The Fables of India,* coyright © 1955, by Joseph Gaer. Illustrated by Randy Monk. Reprinted by permission of Little, Brown and Co.

CONTENTS

CONTENTS

JAPAN

KOREA

LAOS

PERSIA

THAILAND

TIBET

VIETNAM

PREFACE

Folktales have been told since time immemorial. Long before Europe came into being, the people in Asia gathered to tell or listen to the tales of how the earth and sky came to be separated, of why rain follows the cries or activities of certain birds, of kings and heroes, of demons and monsters, of foxes and stepmothers. Orally handed down by generations of balladiers and storytellers, these tales were eventually collected and recorded for posterity.

Folktale enthusiasts today are fascinated by the similarities of themes and ideas found in the folklore of different countries. There are, for instance, at least a few hundred Cinderella stories throughout the world; the well-known Japanese tale, "The Rice Cake That Rolled Away," is virtually identical to the English "Johnny-Cake." These world-wide similarities may be explained by the hypothesis that the normal reactions of the human mind to similar situations everywhere produce similar results. However, a study of the detailed forms in which these tales have been told often reveals substantial differences.

A number of European scholars maintain that this phenomenon of identicalness, however superficial, is due to the diffusion of culture from one single civilization. Some of them attempt to find this universal source in a legendary sunken continent, Atlantis. Others look to ancient Egypt, of whose culture and civilization very little is known. Still others believe that the Orient provided the nucleus of stories from which European folktales were derived.

The latter theory, originally advanced by Kohler of Germany, Clouston of England, and Cosquin of France at the turn of the century, has recently been taken up by an increasing number of Asian folklorists who are convinced that classical Asian tales, such as "The Mystery Maiden from Heaven," "The Monkey Gardeners," "The Magic Hammer," and "The Fox's Daughter" were the prototypes of some of the popular European myths, legends, and stories.

Largely due to philological reasons, ancient Asian tales are difficult to translate into English, and thus most American and English translators and retellers of these stories have often missed the delicacy and subtlety which are so evident in the original. For this book, therefore, I have carefully chosen those versions which have captured the humor, wit, and wisdom of Asian folk literature.

I.K.J.

BURMA

THE TALL TALES

There once lived three brothers who were known throughout the land for the tall tales they told. They would travel from place to place telling their strange stories to whoever would listen. No one ever believed their tales and all who heard them would cry out with exclamations of disbelief.

One day while traveling very far from home the three brothers came upon a wealthy prince. The prince was dressed very elegantly and bedecked in jewels such as the three men had never seen in their lives. They thought how wonderful it would be to have such possessions so they devised a plan whereby they could use their storytelling ability to trick the prince out of his belongings.

They said to the prince: "Let's tell each other stories of past adventures and if anyone should doubt the truth of what the other is saying then that person must become a slave to the others." Now the brothers had no use for a slave but if they could make the prince their slave then they could take his clothes because they would then belong to them.

The prince agreed to their plan. The brothers were sure they would win because no one had ever heard their stories without uttering cries of disbelief. And so they found a passer-by and asked him to act as judge in the matter. All sat down under the shade of a tree and the storytelling began.

The first brother stood up to tell his tale. With a smile on his face he began to speak: "When I was a young boy I thought it would be fun to hide from my brothers so I climbed the tallest tree in our village and remained there all day while my brothers searched high and low for me. When night fell my brothers gave up the search and returned home. It was then that I realized that I was unable to climb down the tree. But I knew I could get down with the help of a rope, so I went to the nearest cottage and borrowed a rope and was then able to climb down the tree and return home."

When the prince heard this ridiculous story he did not make a comment but merely stood and waited for the next story to begin. The three brothers were quite surprised but were sure that the second story would not be believed by the prince. And so the second brother began his tale: "That day when my brother hid from us I was searching for him in the forest. I saw something run into the bushes and thinking it was my brother I ran in after it. When I got into the bushes I saw that it was not my brother but a huge hungry tiger. He opened his mouth to devour me and I jumped inside and crawled into his belly before he could chew me up. When inside I started jumping up and down and making loud, fierce noises. The beast did not know what was happening and became so frightened that he spit me out with such force that I traveled several hundred feet through the air and landed back in the middle of our village. And so though I was but a young lad I saved our whole village from the fearful tiger, because never again did the beast come near our village."

After this story the prince once again made no comment. He merely asked that the third story begin. The three brothers were quite upset by this and as the last brother began his tale he had quite a frown upon his face. But he was still quite determined to make up a story so absurd that the prince could not this time help but doubt its truthfulness. And so he began his tale: "One day as I was walking along the banks of the river I saw that all the fishermen seemed quite unhappy. I inquired as to why they seemed so sad. They therefore informed me that they had not caught one fish in a week and their families were going hungry as a result. I told

4

them that I would try and help them. So I dove into the water and was immediately transformed into a fish. I swam around until I saw the source of the problem. A giant fish had eaten all the smaller fish and was himself avoiding the fishermen's nets. When this giant saw me he came toward me and was about to devour me, but I changed back to human form and slashed the fish open with my sword. The fish inside his belly were then able to escape. Many swam right into the waiting nets. When I returned to shore many of the fish were so thankful that I had saved them that they returned with me. When the fishermen saw all these fish jumping onto shore after me they were indeed pleased and rewarded me abundantly."

When this story was finished the prince did not doubt a word of it. The three brothers were quite upset but at least they knew that they not doubt the words of the prince. And so the prince began his tale: "I am a prince of great wealth and property. I am on the road in search of three slaves who have escaped from me. I have searched high and low for them as they were very valuable property. I was about to give up the search when I met you three fellows. But now my search is ended because I have found my missing slaves, because you gentlemen are they."

When the brothers heard these words they were shocked. If they agreed to the prince's story then they were admitting that they were his slaves, but if they doubted what he said then they lost the bet and became his slaves anyway. The brothers were so upset by the cleverness of the prince that they said not a word. The passer-by who was judging the contest nevertheless declared that the prince had won the wager.

The prince did not make slaves of these men but instead allowed them to return to their village with the promise that they would never tell tall tales again. And the three brothers were thereafter known throughout the land for their honesty and truthfulness.

Tanya Lee

THE FISHERMAN AND THE
GATEKEEPER

There once lived a king who, in order to celebrate the birth of his first child, decided to give a great banquet. Kings and noblemen from all the surrounding lands were invited to attend, and the event promised to be one of the most spectacular ever seen in that kingdom.

As the day approached, the court was bursting with activity in preparation for the feast. All the food except the fish was prepared days in advance. The fish was to be the main course, and had to be caught at the last moment so that it would be fresh.

The day before the banquet, after all the guests had arrived, there arose a great storm at sea. None of the fishing boats was able to go out and it seemed as though the king's banquet would be ruined. All the other food would seem like nothing without the main course and the king was very sad at the thought of being disgraced in front of all the visiting nobility.

All seemed lost until the gatekeeper announced that the king had a visitor. The visitor was allowed to enter and in walked a fisherman with a huge net filled to the brim with large and delicious-looking fresh fish. The fisherman had heard of the king's

6

plight and had risked his life and braved the storm to provide fish for the royal banquet.

The king was overcome with happiness at this news. He had the cook prepare the fish at once, and then offered the fisherman any reward he should ask for.

Much to the king's surprise, the fisherman asked for one hundred lashes of the whip. The king was so shocked at this he told the fisherman he could not possibly punish a man who had performed such a brave and wonderful task. But the fisherman insisted that this was the reward he desired, and the king had but to comply. And so the king ordered the one hundred lashes, but he instructed his servants to be very gentle in carrying out the fisherman's strange request.

The servants thought the man must indeed be a fool to ask for such a reward, and they were so gentle that they did not in any way harm the man. After he had received fifty lashes of the whip the fisherman told the servants to stop. He then informed them that the remaining fifty lashes were to go to the gatekeeper with whom he had promised to share his reward.

The servants immediately sent for the king and the fisherman then explained why he wanted to share his reward with the gate-keeper. When the fisherman arrived at the gate with his catch the gatekeeper would not allow him to enter until he promised to share of his reward. And so the fisherman, in order that he might not be delayed in delivering the fish to the king, had immediately agreed to the gatekeeper's request.

The king was very angry when he heard this story. He ordered the servants to give the gatekeeper the fifty remaining lashes, but this time without gentleness. He then had the gatekeeper banished from the kingdom.

As for the fisherman, he was rewarded generously and given a place of honor at the king's banquet. The banquet was a complete success and all agreed that the fish was the most delicious they had ever tasted.

Tanya Lee

CAMBODIA

THE FISH WITH HOOKED NOSES

Every year when the rainy season begins in the land of Cambodia, some strange fish with hooked noses appear in the Mekong River. The old people in the villages say the fish are trying to reach the temple of Buddha to ask forgiveness for the evil deed of their ancestor.

The wicked fish made the mistake of trying to interfere in the marriage of a beautiful young princess and her prince. This is the story of how a fish came to have anything to do with a marriage and how he was punished for his selfishness.

Long ago there lived a beautiful young princess named Lin Min.

She was so lovely that many princes had come from near and far to ask her hand in marriage. But her father loved his only daughter so much he discouraged all her suitors by demanding that they perform impossible tasks.

Lin Min did not mind losing any of these suitors for she had not given her heart to any of them. She was still young and still happy living at home.

One day the young girl who served Lin Min came back from the well where she drew water for the princess with an exciting story to tell. A kind young traveler, as handsome as any god, came to the well and asked her for a drink of water. "He was so kind and noble and when he spoke his thanks for the water his voice was as sweet as the nightingale." The servant girl's description stirred the heart of the princess.

Of course, the servant girl had also told the handsome young prince how beautiful and kind her mistress was. And the thought of asking for her hand in marriage crossed his mind even though he knew the stories about the king's jealousy.

When the servant girl poured water over the head of her mistress, a small hard object dropped in her hair. The princess clutched it in her hand and did not look to see what it was until the servant girl left the room.

When she opened her hand she found a splendid ruby ring. She knew then that the handsome young man must be a prince and took his ring as a sign that he would be the one she would marry.

Lin Min sent the servant girl back down to the well to see if the prince was still there. "Watch what he is doing and try to find out why he is there," she requested.

Meanwhile Shin Nak, the young prince, realized he had lost his ring and was looking for it around the well. When he saw the servant girl he told her about losing the ring. She helped him look for it but they could not find it anywhere.

The servant girl returned to her mistress to report the latest developments and Lin Min told her to return to the well and tell the prince that his ring would be returned by her hand.

He took this as a sign that heaven had indeed intended them to be man and wife and immediately rushed to ask the king for his daughter's hand. Even the king was overwhelmed by the young man's charm and good looks but even so he was not willing to let his daughter marry him unless he could perform the required tasks.

The first task the king required the young man to perform was to gather up every single grain of rice scattered from a basket by his servant. The prince was given only one night to collect the rice and knew he would never be able to do it no matter how much time he had. In a state of despair the prince sat down beneath a tree and wept over his misfortune. Just then a bird came down and sat on his shoulder. "You may not remember but you once saved my life when a hungry cat was about to pounce on me, good prince," said the bird. "Now it is my turn to help you." With that the bird called together all his friends and they flew about over the fields until they had collected all the rice.

The king could scarcely believe it when the rice was counted and all the grains were found to be there. But still he was not satisfied. Next he asked his servants to scatter little white pebbles in the river and gave the prince one night to collect them. Once again despairing the prince sat down on the bank of the river. Then a fish popped up out of the water and spoke to him. "Last year you released me from the fisherman's hook and set me free. Now I will help you." And he asked all the fish to gather up the white pebbles. When the pebbles had been gathered it turned out that one fish was keeping a stone in his mouth. The other fish scolded him and made him feel ashamed so he swam over to offer it to the prince. When the prince took the stone from his mouth he accidentally pushed against the fish's nose bending it into a hooked shape. Everyone said that was the fish's punishment for being greedy and to this day the descendants of that fish have hooked noses.

The king was once again amazed and was just about ready to give up his daughter. The final task was simply to pick the hand of the princess from the hands of all the other women in the court.

All the women stood behind a screen and put one hand through a hole in the screen. This turned out to be the easiest task of all because the princess wore the ruby ring so the prince recognized her hand at once.

Now that all the tasks were successfully completed the king gave up his daughter with good grace. He ordered a huge wedding feast prepared for the young couple and they lived happily together for many years.

Tanya Lee

CHINA

THE TREASURE OF LI-PO

Li-Po, the basket-maker, lived all alone on the banks of the Yangtse River, far away from towns and the busy world. In fact, he was some distance even from the nearest village, and he hardly ever went into it, but every morning and every evening he looked toward it, and seeing the smoke from the cooking stoves and the little lights in the houses, he would say: "Well, we are both getting old, and neither of us is very big or very rich, but we are managing to hold our own, I think. We are not doing too badly." And then he would rub his hands together and chuckle, for he was a simple old man, and kind and good, and although he did not see anyone from the village for months at a time, he wished them all well.

Twice a year, a merchant came from a far-off city to buy the baskets he made from the bamboos on the banks of the river. He stayed one night with Li-Po in his hut and his servants slept in tents around it. So poor and small was the hut that you might say for that night the servants were housed better than their master, but the merchant was fond of Li-Po, and thought his conversation and his kindness made up for the very simple entertainment which was all he could offer. In the morning he paid him and loaded the baskets onto his traveling wagon and off they all went, leaving the old man alone again for another six months.

Now it happened one day shortly before the merchant was due to arrive, that a notion came into Li-Po's head to count his money. He kept it in a sack under his bed and each time the merchant paid him he pushed the new coins in along with the old ones and thought no more about them, for he had little need of money. He grew his own vegetables and caught fish in the river and pumped his drink from the well in the courtyard. Living that quiet life, one coat lasted him for a long time. What did he want with money? But he had been making baskets for fifty years, and even small pay mounts up in that time; when he began to pull out the sack, it was so heavy he could hardly move it.

"Here's a business," he said to himself, "there's a terrible weight here."

At last he got it out, and then he found that the sack had lain there for so long that the rats had nibbled a large hole in it, and he had to go creeping under the bed to gather up the stray coins.

"Sharp teeth," he said, "but not sharp wits, for what good is money to a rat? And, for that matter," he added, as he counted it, "what good is money to me?"

He was quite dismayed when he found how much there was, and he sat for a while beside the pile on the floor wondering what to do. But after some time he had an idea which pleased him very much, and he chuckled to himself as he found a new sack and tied the money up securely and then went out to look for the approach of the merchant.

Presently a cloud of dust appeared on the horizon, and soon he saw the wagon and could make out the figure of his friend riding ahead of it. Then all was bustle in his quiet home—buckets of water drawn from the well for the thirsty beasts; rice cakes and a freshly cooked fish set out for the merchant, an old fan taken down from the wall for him to refresh himself with after the dusty ride, and Li-Po standing on the edge of his little property to greet him.

When the meal was eaten the merchant asked Li-Po to share with him a bottle of the wine he always carried on his journeys, and they went out onto the veranda and filled their cups and drank and watched the sun set over the river. The water lilies were closing for the night; nothing moved except a long-legged heron which

18

walked slowly down to the river bank and then stood like a statue, watching for fish.

"It is very peaceful here," said the merchant. "In some ways I envy your lot."

"Yes, it is peaceful," said Li-Po, who had never lived anywhere else, "but I have something on my mind and I want to ask your advice, as a man who has seen much of the world."

"Now what can you possibly have to worry you?" asked the merchant, smiling to himself under his long mustache. "For I will gladly help you in any way I can."

"It is a question of money," said Li-Po.

The merchant was so surprised at hearing the old man say he had some trouble connected with money that he found nothing to say, and Li-Po was always very slow in his thoughts and his speech, so they sat in silence for some time. The merchant lit his pipe and watched the sunset, and at last Li-Po spoke again.

"I should like you to tell me," he said, "the name of the most virtuous and accomplished young lady you have met in your travels."

"That is easy," said the merchant, although he did not see what this could have to do with Li-Po's troubles. "Of all the ladies I have met the most virtuous and accomplished is undoubtedly Miss Ch'en Hua. She lives in the town of Honan, in the house of her father, and her heart is entirely inclined toward goodness. Her embroidery work is the admiration of all her acquaintance, and she plays upon the lute in the most ravishing manner. In addition to this she is so beautiful that a large crowd is always standing at her father's gates in the hope that their eyes will be rewarded by simply seeing her go in or out."

"Good, good," said Li-Po, grunting and chuckling. "Now, my friend, I have a favor to ask of you. It happens that I have a great deal of money which I do not want. Will you take it when you go away tomorrow, and buy a jewel with it, and give it to Miss Ch'en Hua with the good wishes of one who admires virtue far more than he cares for money?"

"Certainly I will," said the merchant, "but allow me to say that I am surprised to hear you have so much money to spare, and I wonder whether it would not be wiser for you to keep it in case you are ever ill or in need."

"No," said Li-Po, "for myself, I shall trust, as I have always trusted, in Providence. But money lying in my house gives me a heavy feeling about the heart. It is not suitable for me to be rich."

"Very well," said the merchant, "I shall do as you ask."

And the next morning when the wagon set out again he took Li-Po's sack of money with him, carefully strapped on his own saddle.

Li-Po had begged him to take a share of it as payment for his trouble, but he was a rich man, and besides he was too fond of Li-Po to count a service done for him as tiresome, so he spent every coin in the sack on a little necklace of carved green jade. He took it with him the next time he visited the town of Honan, and went straight to the house of Miss Ch'en Hua's father.

"You must have an interesting life," said the father, as they sat drinking tea. "You see a great deal of the world."

"I see some strange things," said the merchant. He smiled at Miss Ch'en Hua, who sat beside her father, and took the necklace out of his wallet and handed it to her. "What, for instance, do you say to this? I have been asked to give it to you with the good wishes of someone who lives far from here and who has never seen you, but who admires virtue far more than he cares for money."

"Oh, oh," said Miss Ch'en Hua, covering her face with her hands, for she was as modest as she was beautiful.

"Well, really," said her father, taking the necklace out of her lap to examine it, "it is a fine piece of work. The giver must be a man of taste."

The merchant did not say he had chosen it himself, because he wanted Li-Po to have all the credit for the gift. Presently he was pleased to see Miss Ch'en Hua fasten it around her neck.

When his visit was over and he was standing in the courtyard waiting for his horse to be brought for him, Miss Ch'en Hua came out of the house carrying a packet.

"Please give this small present to the person who sent the jade necklace," she said, "and say that it comes from one who admires a generous heart far more than she cares for jewels." Then, pressing the packet into the merchant's hands and veiling her blushes with her fan, she went quickly into the house.

"Now this is getting rather complicated," said the merchant to himself. "I very much doubt whether my old friend Li-Po will know what to do with a present from Miss Ch'en Hua."

However, he was anxious to deliver it, and one day a little later when his business took him near to where Li-Po lived, he rode over to the old man's hut.

When Li-Po saw him coming he ran to meet him, surprised at seeing him again so soon.

"I have not made enough baskets yet for it to be worth your while to come," he said.

"It is not baskets which bring me here," said the merchant. "I have been entrusted with a present for you."

"A present," said Li-Po, in dismay. "Who would send me a present?"

"Miss Ch'en Hua, to whom I gave a carved jade necklace from you, sends you this with good wishes from one who admires a generous heart far more than she loves jewels," said the merchant, handing the packet to Li-Po.

Li-Po found the silken strings difficult to untie, because his hands were roughened with hard work, but at last he managed it, and the wrappings fell off and they saw a most beautiful scarf band embroidered all over in silk of every color with little figures of noble youths at play.

"It is the work of her own hands," said the merchant. "No one is her equal for embroidery."

"Alas," said Li-Po, touching the silk gently for fear of spoiling it, "this is a present fit for a gallant prince. I should be ashamed to have such a beautiful thing. Tell me," he said, "the name of the most generous and noble young man you have met in your travels."

"That is easy," said the merchant. "Of all the youths I have met the most generous and noble is undoubtedly the young lord Yuan-Sen. He lives in the town of Yunan, and the people who are under his rule are the happiest in the world."

"Good, good," said Li-Po. "Then, my friend, I beg you will take this scarf band to him with the good wishes of one who admires a generous heart."

"Very well," said the merchant, thinking that after all it was a pity the beautiful embroidery should not be used, "I shall take it to him."

And, sure enough, soon after, he went to the province of Yunan and took Miss Ch'en Hua's packet and gave it to the young lord Yuan-Sen with "the good wishes of one who admires a generous heart."

"This is very strange," said Yuan-Sen, unfolding the packet. "I do not understand why I should be given such a present—" for he was as modest as he was noble. When he unwrapped the packet and saw the embroidered scarf band, he blushed and said, "This is the gift of a lady, and she must have the most beautiful fingers in the world, for never have I seen its equal."

Now the merchant did not like to say that it was really the gift of a poor old man who wore the same blue coat year after year and whose fingers were rough and coarse with basket-making, so he smiled and said nothing.

But Yuan-Sen was not willing to let matters rest at that, and when the merchant was leaving he sent for him and showed him an enormous collection of parcels and packages each stamped with his own mark, a crescent moon and a phoenix.

"I wish you to take these as an offering to the giver of the scarf band," he said, "and say they come with the good wishes of one who admires the skill of hands more than all the treasures in his province."

"I shall have to get an extra horse to carry that load," said the merchant.

"I shall give you a horse for your trouble," said the lordly Yuan-Sen, and a fine horse was led up and all the parcels were loaded onto it and securely tied.

The merchant rode at once with the treasures to Li-Po on the banks of the Yangtse River.

The old man was surprised to see him coming and when he heard his story he wrung his hands in despair.

"Let us see what he has sent you, at all events," said the merchant. He untied one of the parcels, and then even he, who had seen so much of the world, fell back with a loud exclamation of surprise, and as for Li-Po, he covered his eyes with his hands as if he was not fit even to look at the treasures it contained—gold and silver drinking cups, birds and fishes carved out of precious stones, painted ivory screens, they lay in a heap at their feet on the mud floor of Li-Po's hut.

"It is not mine, it is not mine!" cried Li-Po.

"It is yours," said the merchant. "The lord Yuan-Sen gave it with the good wishes of one who admires the skill of hands more than all the treasures in his province. And no one can deny," he added slyly, "that you have great skill in your hands and much practice in using it after fifty years in making baskets. Li-Po, you are now a very rich man."

He bent down to undo another parcel, but Li-Po stopped him.

"No, no," he said, "leave the rest. Let us tie this one up again, and then, my friend, I beg you to take it away and give it to Miss Ch'en Hua with the same message as the lord Yuan-Sen sent to me. But please take something out of it to repay you for your trouble."

"Very well," said the merchant, "I will do as you say, but I am afraid this business is going to have a bad ending. And, as I shall have to neglect my other work to go to the town of Honan, I shall take this silver cup to repay me for my time, though you know I am always glad to serve you."

Li-Po thanked him and they tied up the parcel of treasures again and the merchant set off for the town of Honan.

As soon as he got there he went straight to the house of Miss Ch'en Hua's father and led the horse loaded with presents into the courtyard. Then he called to Miss Ch'en Hua to come and see what he had brought.

"You have a great load of merchandise there," said Miss Ch'en Hua's father, coming into the courtyard with his daughter. "Where are you going to sell it?"

"I am not going to sell it," said the merchant. "It is for Miss Ch'en Hua, with the good wishes of one who admires the skill of hands more than all the treasures in his province."

Without thinking, he had given the whole of Yuan-Sen's message, and as soon as he said it he bit his lip, so that he should not smile when he remembered that all the treasures which Li-Po owned in *his* province were the sun and the wind and the water

23

lilies on the Yangtse River, and when Miss Ch'en Hua's father said, "Which is the province of the giver of this princely gift?" he answered, still with his mind full of Li-Po, "The Yangtse Province." Miss Ch'en Hua and her father were amazed at the magnificent present, and when the parcels and packets were unwrapped they were so overcome that for some time they could not speak.

"Now I have done my duty, and I must go," said the merchant, who was beginning to feel uneasy about the whole business, but Miss Ch'en Hua's father put his hand on his arm and held him back.

"Not so fast," he said, "not so fast. I see now what all this means." He turned to his daughter who was still staring as if she was in a dream at the gold and silver and jade and ivory and precious silks which filled the whole courtyard. "It is quite clear that this present comes from a great lord," he said. "See, here is his emblem on the wrappings—a crescent moon and a phoenix —no one but a great lord would have such an emblem, and it is quite clear too that he wishes to marry you. Really, I think, my dear child, that you could not do better. What do you say?"

Miss Ch'en Hua answered in a trembling voice that she would like to see the giver of the present before anything was decided.

"Very well," said her father, "we shall pay a visit to this princely young man in the Yangtse Province. You must guide us to his palace," he said to the merchant, who trembled in his shoes and wished he had never had anything to do with Li-Po or Yuan-Sen or Miss Ch'en Hua. "We shall start in a month from this day; that will give me time to prepare, for we must go in state and we must take some rich offerings. Do not forget," he said, fixing the merchant sternly with his eye, rather annoyed with him for not showing more interest in the scheme, "in a month from this day you must be in the courtyard to guide us, and mind, if you do not come, I shall ruin your trade in this town and in the eight towns round about it."

"Oh, Father," cried Miss Ch'en Hua, "do not speak so harshly to our kind friend who has brought this honor to me," and she bent down and gathered up gold and silver ornaments and pressed them on the merchant until his arms were full.

He blessed her and packed them on his horse, but do what he would, he could not speak with enthusiasm about the expedition to the Yangtse River. His heart sank when he thought of Li-Po's poor hut, with nothing in it but an old bed and one old table, and the rice cakes and the fish and the well-water which were the most he could provide for his guests. He did not know what was to be done. However, Miss Ch'en Hua's father was a powerful man, so he had to promise that in a month's time he would be in the courtyard and would guide them to the home of the unknown giver of presents in the Yangtse Province.

Then, as he was turning away, wondering how he could break the news to Li-Po, Miss Ch'en Hua came up to him while her father was busy watching the servants carry the treasure into the house. She gave him a parcel and said: "Please give it to the one who sent me the present and say I hope he will wear it at our meeting," and although the merchant had had more than enough of this business of presents, he could not refuse Miss Ch'en Hua, because she looked so beautiful, blushing and smiling and bowing in front of him. So he took the parcel and turned his horse's head and rode as fast as he could, day and night, to Li-Po in the Yangtse Province.

The old man came out to meet him; this time he guessed that the visit must have something to do with the presents and his face was full of anxiety before the merchant had even alighted from his horse.

"We are ruined," said the merchant. "Miss Ch'en Hua's father is a proud man, and powerful. He will never forgive me if I do not bring him here, and when he comes, what will you do?"

Li-Po wrung his hands. "Alas," he said, "I am thinking of the beautiful and accomplished Miss Ch'en Hua. When she finds an old man in a poor hut at the end of her journey she will think a cruel trick has been played on her. There is only one thing I can do, my friend, to spare her this shame. I must die."

"Do not speak like that," said the merchant. "We must think of a plan." But he could not think of anything.

"She sent you this," he said at last, giving Li-Po Miss Ch'en Hua's parcel, "and I was to say that she hoped the giver of the presents would wear it at the meeting."

With trembling hands Li-Po untied the silken strings and unwrapped an embroidered silk coat suitable for a nobleman to wear in the flower of his youth. He groaned and his tears ran down.

"Now we see how cruelly she has been deceived," he said. "She will die of shame when she comes here. But take it to the young lord Yuan-Sen, so at least it will have a worthy owner. And then if no plan occurs to you, you must keep your word and go back to meet Miss Ch'en Hua's father."

"But what will you do?" asked the merchant. "Promise me that you will think no more of dying."

Li-Po shook his head. "I am a foolish old man," he said. "I should have died long ago before I brought shame upon the beautiful and virtuous Miss Ch'en Hua." And as that was all he would say, the merchant left him and took the coat to the young lord Yuan-Sen. But he had not the heart to make up a message, and when Yuan-Sen began to exclaim about the lovely coat and to ask questions about its maker, he told him the whole story about Li-Po and the sack of money, and how one thing had led to another until at last the old man was sitting in his little hut grieving and wishing he might die.

"So the one thing I must not do is to send a gift of any kind," said Yuan-Sen, smiling. "You and he have both had enough to do with gifts."

"That is true," said the merchant.

"And yet it will look strange if you go back to meet Miss Ch'en Hua and to guide her to the Yangtse Province and take no offering in your hand. You had better give her this ring." And he handed the merchant a gold ring set with an emerald as big as a pigeon's egg.

The merchant took the ring, though he did not see that it mattered much whether he brought a present or not, when the end of the journey was bound to be so disappointing.

"My advice to you," went on Yuan-Sen, "is to say nothing to the father or to Miss Ch'en Hua, but simply to bring them to where the old man lives. Who knows? God may help the simple-hearted in a way you cannot guess."

So the merchant rode off, and as he had not thought of any plan, he did not go back to Li-Po but went straight to Honan to meet Miss Ch'en Hua and her father.

26

Li-Po sat on the banks of the Yangtse River, too unhappy to do his basket work, and too poor to make any preparations for his guests. Each day as he watched the sun set, he thought: "Now we are one day nearer to the meeting. If I do not die before then, I shall die of shame on that morning." And he forgot to look toward the village with his blessing, and could not take pleasure in the water lilies or the herons or any of the things which used to please him.

At last, one day, when he looked up from his sad brooding, he saw a huge cloud of dust on the horizon and soon he made out the shapes of many men on horseback and a great number of wagons. "Alas, alas," he cried, running to and fro in his grief, "they are coming a full day before their time, and here am I, still alive!" He went into his hut and sat with his head bowed on his hands. He tried not to hear the sound of the arrival of the horses and wagons, though the air was full of the merry shouts of the riders and drivers. He buried his head in his arms and tried not to hear or to see. Then someone came into the hut and he felt a hand on his shoulder, and thinking it must be his friend the merchant, he looked up with a groan. A young man of the handsomest and noblest appearance was standing there smiling at him.

"What can you want with me?" asked Li-Po.

"I want you to adopt me," said the young man, still smiling and still keeping his hand on Li-Po's shoulder.

"Alas, it is a sad thing that so gallant a young man must be mad," said Li-Po.

The young man laughed. "I am not mad," he said. "Li-Po, I am the lord Yuan-Sen and I know all about your trouble and have come to deliver you from it. Listen, you must adopt me as your nephew, and then when Miss Ch'en Hua and her father come I shall wear the coat and scarf she sent and you will say you gave them to me because they were more suitable for a young man than an old one."

"Still that will not save her," said Li-Po. "What will she think when she finds herself in this poor hut?"

"Come outside and you shall see something," said the young man, smiling more broadly than ever. "But first tell me," he went on, shaking Li-Po's shoulder a little, "will you have me for a nephew?"

"I should be proud to have such a fine youth for my nephew," said Li-Po, with a faint hope arising in his heart, and they embraced as relations do.

Then they went outside the hut together and Li-Po gasped with surprise. All the men whom Yuan-Sen had brought with him were busily at work building the most magnificent pavilion out of materials they had brought with them in the wagons. Some of them were clearing the ground for the polished floors to rest on, others were unpacking the red lacquer which was to make the walls. They had already set up a peal of golden bells where the entrance was to be, and were unloading chests containing rich carpets and silks and fine silver drinking cups and china plates and big gold dishes, and crates of rare and delicate food and precious wine.

"We shall not lack for anything in our entertainment, Uncle," said Yuan-Sen. "Before sunset everything will be in place, and tomorrow morning you must put on this gold robe and this crimson cap to do honor to your guests."

"Nay," said Li-Po, "I think, Nephew, I had better put it on now, for I shall need some practice in wearing a golden robe and a crimson cap."

The next morning the carriages and horses of Miss Ch'en Hua's father were drawing near to the place where Li-Po had his hut. The merchant rode a little ahead of them, because he was so anxious and unhappy; he was not only afraid of the revenge Miss Ch'en Hua's father would take on him when he found a poor old man instead of a rich young one, but also he was afraid that Li-Po might no longer be alive. So he looked eagerly for the first sight of the little hut, as if that in itself could tell him something. He looked, and then rubbed his eyes and looked again. He thought his mind must be giving way, or that he had missed the road, although he knew it as well as the road to his own house, for there, a few hundred yards away, stood a rose-colored pavilion with green lattice verandas and a gilt roof, and even at this distance he could hear the sweet peal of golden bells ringing in welcome.

Miss Ch'en Hua's father rode up and joined him. "It is a fine-looking house," he said.

"It is indeed," said the merchant, staring, and wishing he could gallop quickly in advance of the others to find out what mysterious thing had happened.

"I think I can see our host at the gate," said Miss Ch'en Hua's father, and the merchant narrowed his eyes and looked, and sure enough, there stood his old friend Li-Po dressed in a gorgeous robe which glittered in the morning sunlight, and a crimson cap on his head. The merchant nearly fell off his horse with surprise and joy. Then he saw another person come out of the pavilion and stand beside Li-Po. He wore the embroidered coat Miss Ch'en Hua had sent, and the merchant soon recognized him to be the lordly and gallant Yuan-Sen. It was all he could do not to throw up his cap and shout, for now he understood everything and it was as perfect as the best dream he had ever had in his life.

They woke Miss Ch'en Hua, who had been sleeping in her carriage, and she smoothed her lovely hair and put on the emerald ring the merchant had brought for her, and then they rode up to the gate and Li-Po ran forward to greet them with Yuan-Sen at his side, and they all went into the pavilion to the gay sound of the bells and of many stringed instruments.

It was love at first sight with the young lord Yuan-Sen and Miss Ch'en Hua. Her father gladly gave his consent to their marriage, Li-Po gave his as gladly, and no one took a livelier part in the rejoicings at the wedding than the merchant.

At last the time came for the father to go home again and for the two young people to leave for Yuan-Sen's province. They took tender farewells of Li-Po, and Yuan-Sen, leading him a little apart from the rest, said: "Uncle, I wish to leave a number of servants behind to look after you in the red pavilion, and also enough money for you to be comfortable there."

"I beg you to do nothing of the kind," said Li-Po. "Your society and the society of Miss Ch'en Hua, now your wife, has been very pleasant to me, but once you have gone I wish to go back to my old style of living. Believe me, Nephew, there was never a more contented man than I was in my hut. I should not know what to do with either servants or money. In fact, I ask you as a last favor to bid some of your servants stay behind to remove the red pavilion, for I should not enjoy it alone."

"I must do as you say, Uncle," said Yuan-Sen, "but I wish I

29

might have had my way. Once a year I shall come to visit you, and the hut which shelters you will always be fine enough for me."

They embraced with great affection, as relations do. Then Yuan-Sen joined his bride and they set off for the province of Yunan, and the father went back to Honan, and the merchant rode away somewhere on his business. But before *he* left Li-Po said, "I shall expect to see you in six months' time, as usual."

"I shall be glad to come," said the merchant, "but what use will you have for my services now?"

"Why, to sell my baskets, of course!" said Li-Po, staring at him in surprise.

The servants whom Yuan-Sen left behind made haste to pull down and pack up the red lacquer pavilion and the silks and carpets and fine china. Soon they loaded it up on wagons and then they too were gone.

But the young lord Yuan-Sen had not been able after all to leave Li-Po as poor as he had found him. "I cannot bear it," he said to himself, "though I am afraid he will not be pleased." And so he had hidden a sack of money under Li-Po's bed.

When the old man found it, he thought at first it was his old sack of coins, come back again by magic, but when he opened it and saw that they were gold this time instead of copper, he guessed who had put it there and he shook his head and grunted, but in the end he smiled.

"My nephew is very clever," he said, "but I am cleverer still. Last time I spent my money far afield. This time I shall spend it nearer home." And he loaded the sack onto his old wheelbarrow and trundled it over to the village which he used to look at in the morning and the evening. He called to the headman to come out and he gave him the sack of coins to spend on the poor people, "So that no one shall ever be cold and hungry in this village again," he said.

The headman of the village was a good man and he rejoiced. "It is a small village," he said, "but there was suffering in the cold weather last year; with this enormous sum of money that need never happen again. We wondered some time ago to see a red lacquer palace go up beside your hut," he added with a shy smile, "but now it has gone again."

"Yes," said Li-Po, also smiling shyly, "now it has gone again. I must go home because I have lost a good deal of time lately and I am behind in my basket work."

But Li-Po's name was blessed ever after by all the people in that village, and Yuan-Sen and his wife loved him to the end of his days.

Alice Ritchie

HOK LEE AND THE DWARFS

There once lived in a small town in China a man name Hok Lee. He was a steady, industrious man, who not only worked hard at his trade, but did all his own housework as well, for he had no wife to do it for him.

"What an excellent, industrious man is this Hok Lee!" his neighbors said. "How hard he works. He never leaves his house to amuse himself or to take a holiday as others do!"

But Hok Lee was by no means the virtuous person his neighbors thought him. True, he worked hard enough by day, but at night, when all respectable folk were fast asleep, he would steal out and join a dangerous band of robbers who broke into rich people's houses and carried off all they could lay their hands on. This state of things went on for some time, and though a thief was caught now and then and punished, no suspicion ever fell on Hok Lee, he was such a *very* respectable, hard-working man.

He had already amassed a good store of money as his share of the proceeds of these robberies when it happened one morning on going to market that a neighbor said to him, "Why, Hok Lee, what is the matter with your face? One side of it is all swelled up."

True enough, Hok Lee's right cheek was twice the size of his left, and it soon began to feel very uncomfortable.

"I will bind up my face," Hok Lee said. "Doubtless the warmth will cure the swelling."

Next day, however, it was only worse, and day by day it grew bigger and bigger till it was nearly as large as his head and very painful. Hok Lee was at his wits' end what to do. Not only was his cheek unsightly and painful, but his neighbors began to jeer and make fun of him, which hurt his feelings very much indeed.

One day, as luck would have it, a traveling doctor came to the town. He sold not only all kinds of medicine but also dealt in many strange charms against witches and evil spirits. Hok Lee determined to consult him and asked him into his house.

After the doctor had examined him carefully, he said, "This, oh, Hok Lee, is no ordinary swollen face. I strongly suspect you have been doing some wrong deed which has called down the anger of the spirits on you. None of my drugs will cure you, but if you are willing to pay me handsomely, I will tell you how you may be cured."

Then Hok Lee and the doctor began to bargain, and it was a long time before they could come to terms. The doctor got the better of it in the end, for he was determined not to part with his secret under a certain price, and Hok Lee had no mind to carry his huge cheek about with him to the end of his days. So he was obliged to part with the greater portion of his ill-gotten gains. When the doctor had pocketed the money, he told Hok Lee to go on the first night of the full moon to a certain wood and there to watch by a particular tree. After a time the dwarfs and sprites who live underground would come out to dance. When they saw him they would be sure to make him dance too.

"And mind you dance your very best," added the doctor. "If you dance well and please them, they will allow you to present a petition and you can then beg to be cured; but if you dance badly, they will most likely do you some mischief out of spite." With that he took his leave and departed.

Happily, the first night of the full moon was near, and at the proper time Hok Lee set out for the wood. With a little trouble he found the tree the doctor had described, and feeling nervous, he climbed up into it. He had hardly settled himself on a branch when in the moonlight he saw the dwarfs assembling. They came from

33

all sides until at length there appeared to be hundreds of them. They seemed in high glee, and danced and skipped and capered about, while Hok Lee grew so eager watching them that he crept farther and farther along his branch until it gave a loud crack. All the dwarfs stood still, and Hok Lee felt as if his heart stood still also.

Then one of the dwarfs called out, "Someone is up in that tree. Come down at once, whoever you are, or we must come and fetch you!"

In great terror, Hok Lee proceeded to come down, but he was so nervous that, just before he reached the ground, he tripped and came rolling down in the most absurd manner. When he had picked himself up, he came forward with a low bow, and the dwarf who had first spoken and who appeared to be the leader, said, "Now, then, who are you, and what brings you here?"

So Hok Lee told him the sad story of his swollen cheek, and how he had been advised to come to the forest and beg the dwarfs to cure him.

"It is well," replied the dwarf. "We will see about that. First, however, you must dance for us. Should your dancing please us, perhaps we may be able to do something, but should you dance badly, we shall assuredly punish you; so now take warning and dance away."

With that, he and all the other dwarfs sat down in a large ring, leaving Hok Lee to dance alone in the middle. He felt half frightened to death and, besides, was much shaken by his fall from the tree, and he did not feel at all inclined to dance. But the dwarfs were not to be trifled with.

"Begin!" cried their leader, and, "Begin!" shouted the rest in chorus.

In despair Hok Lee began to dance. First he hopped on one foot and then on the other, but he was so stiff and so nervous that he made but a poor attempt, and after a time sank down on the ground and vowed he could dance no more.

The dwarfs were very angry. They crowded around Hok Lee and abused him. "You come here to be cured, indeed!" they cried. "You have brought one big cheek with you, but you shall take away two." With that they ran off and disappeared, leaving Hok Lee to find his way home as best he might.

He hobbled away, weary and depressed, and not a little anxious because of the dwarf's threat. Nor were his fears unfounded, for when he rose next morning his left cheek was swelled up as big as his right, and he could hardly see out of his puffy eyes. Hok Lee was in despair, and his neighbors jeered at him more than ever. The doctor had disappeared, so there was nothing for it but to try the dwarfs once more.

He waited a month until the first night of the full moon came around again, and then he trudged back to the forest and sat down under the tree from which he had fallen. He had not long to wait. Before long the dwarfs came trooping out until all were assembled.

"I do not feel quite easy," said one. "I feel as if some horrid human being were near us."

When Hok Lee heard this, he came forward and bowed down to the ground before the dwarfs, who came crowding around and laughed heartily at his comical appearance with his two big cheeks.

"What do you want now?" they asked.

Hok Lee proceeded to tell them of his fresh misfortunes and begged so hard to be allowed one more attempt at dancing that the dwarfs consented, for there is nothing they love so much as being amused. Now Hok Lee knew how much depended on his dancing well. He plucked up a good spirit and began, first slowly, then faster by degrees, and he danced so well and so gracefully and invented such new and wonderful steps that the dwarfs were quite delighted with him.

They clapped their tiny hands and shouted, "Well done, Hok Lee, well done. Go on, dance some more."

And Hok Lee danced on and on until he really could dance no more and was obliged to stop.

Then the leader of the dwarfs said, "We are well pleased, Hok Lee, and as a recompense for your dancing your face shall be cured. Farewell."

With these words he and the other dwarfs vanished, and Hok Lee, putting his hands to his face, found to his great joy that his cheeks were now their natural size. The way home seemed short

35

and easy, and he went to bed happy, and he resolved never to go out robbing again.

Next day the whole town was full of the news of his sudden cure. His neighbors questioned him but could get nothing from him except that he had discovered a wonderful cure for all kinds of diseases.

After a time a rich neighbor, who had been ill for some years, came and offered Hok Lee a large sum of money if he would tell him how he might be cured. Hok Lee consented on condition that the neighbor would swear to keep the secret. He did so, and Hok Lee told him of the dwarfs and their dances.

The neighbor went off, carefully obeyed Hok Lee's directions, and was duly cured by the dwarfs. Then another and another came to Hok Lee to beg his secret, and from each he extracted a vow of secrecy and a large sum of money. This went on for some years, so that at length Hok Lee became a very wealthy man and ended his days in peace and prosperity.

Pearl S. Buck and Lyle Kenyon Engel

THE FOX'S DAUGHTER

Nothing is luckier than to be the child of a fox, for, without taking the trouble to learn anything, foxes know as much magic as the man who spends his whole life studying it, and when a fox's child takes human form, as sometimes happens, and becomes a boy or a girl, he knows as much magic as his father.

Liu was a young student who should have been working hard for his examinations, but he was rather idle and much preferred wandering about his father's estate, or sailing in a boat on the river which ran through it, to sitting indoors over his books.

One day, when he was occupied—if it can be called occupied—in this way, he saw the form of a young girl among the reeds which grew upon a little island in the river. Quickly he jumped into his boat and hurried across the water, and, tying the boat up to a willow tree, he began to search the island for her.

For some time he saw nothing, but he heard mocking laughter to the right and to the left, and, running wildly first in one direction and then in the other, he tore his silk robe and broke the strap of one of his sandals. At last he succeeded in running her down, but she looked so beautiful, leaning against a tree and smiling at him, that even after he had got his breath back he could not speak.

"Alas," said the girl in a clear low voice, looking at his torn robe and flapping sandal, "if Master Liu pursued his studies with the same zeal as he has pursued me, he would take a high place when the candidates go up to the Examination Hall, and some day he would be a man of great importance—but of course he will do nothing of the sort."

Liu eagerly asked her name and how she happened to know all about him, and also how she came to be upon the island, for he could see no boat except his own.

"My name is Feng-Lien," said the maiden, "but as to how I came here, I shall not tell you, and I can go away again as swiftly."

(This was not surprising, because, of course, she was a fox's daughter, and could appear and disappear at will.) And now she made a movement as if she meant to go, but Liu sprang forward with his hands spread out.

"I beg you to stay," he cried, "or at least tell me where we shall meet again, for you are the most beautiful person I have ever seen."

"Look for me in your books," said the maiden; then, seeing his face become clouded with disappointment, she took a little silver mirror from her girdle and gave it to him. "There," she said, "you shall have something which has belonged to me, but I warn you, you will never see me in it except through your books." And in a moment she had vanished.

Liu went back to his boat feeling very sad, and many times before he reached the house he looked longingly into the silver mirror, but all he saw was the back view of the beautiful Feng-Lien standing as if she was watching someone going away from her.

As soon as he reached his room, remembering what she had said, he took out the heavy and difficult books which he had never had a mind to study, and laying them on the top of the mirror, he tried to see it through them, but of course he saw nothing, not even its silver handle, buried under those great volumes.

"Feng-Lien meant more than she said," he remarked to himself, and he removed the books from the mirror with a sigh and applied himself earnestly to reading them, refusing to see his friends when they came to the house and not accepting any invitations. After he had spent several days in this way, he looked into the mirror again, and there was Feng-Lien with her face turned toward him, smiling and nodding as if she was pleased.

For a month or more he did nothing but study, looking often

into the mirror to be encouraged by the lovely face of Feng-Lien, but presently the fine summer weather came, and he could not force himself to stay in the house. He began once more to wander about the garden and the wild land beside the river, idly enjoying the scent of the newly opened flowers and the sight of the bright birds.

"Perhaps I shall see Feng-Lien again," he said. But he did not find her, and in his heart he knew she would not come while he behaved in this way. Then, one evening, after he had been on a fishing expedition all day with some friends, when he pulled out the silver mirror he saw Feng-Lien crying bitterly, and the next morning she had her back turned to him.

"It is clear that there is only one thing to be done," he said to himself. "I must make a habit of working all the time."

He took the silver mirror and nailed it on the wall so that whenever he raised his eyes from his difficult reading he would see Feng-Lien's face. She always looked happy now. This went on for two years, and at the end of that time he went up to the Examination Hall and did so well that he took a high place in the final list.

"Now," he said, "at last, I shall surely be allowed to see Feng-Lien herself."

He took up the mirror and looked for a long time at her reflection, at the arched eyebrows and the beautiful eyes and the smiling mouth, until it seemed to him that her lips parted and she spoke, yes, she seemed to be speaking words of welcome and congratulation, and suddenly the mirror dissolved into a drop of dew and instead of her likeness, Feng-Lien herself stood before him.

"Really," she said, bowing very low, "I am quite frightened of this learned young man."

"The success I have had is entirely owing to you," said Liu.

So they were married, and Liu attained to one of the highest positions in China, but Feng-Lien never again had to use the magic she possessed by reason of being a fox's daughter. She found quite simple ways of keeping her husband, who continued to be by nature somewhat lazy, up to the mark.

Alice Ritchie

THE MYSTERY MAIDEN FROM
HEAVEN

Once upon a time there was a poor young shepherd named Hu Min who lived all alone in a mountain hut. Each day he went out to tend his sheep and each night he returned to his lonely hut.

Sometimes he sat in front of the fire and dreamed that he had a lovely maiden to spend the long lonely nights with him.

From time to time he walked down the mountain to a nearby village to buy his rice and the few other things he might be able to afford.

One day when he went to the market a traveling merchant was there selling a beautiful hand-painted scroll. The scroll was the finest silk and the dark-haired maiden painted on it so beautiful that Hu Min could not take his eyes off her.

He was so much in love with the maiden in the painting that he ran straight home and dug up his savings of 500 won and ran all the way back to the village again with the money.

He took the scroll home and hung it up over his mat so the maiden could watch over him while he slept. Every day he made a small offering of food to the picture.

For some time things went on as usual except that just having the picture made Hu Min feel happier.

40

Then one night when he returned from the field his dinner was already cooked and waiting for him on the table. He was very frightened but finally decided he should eat it lest he offend whatever spirits put it there.

The food was the most delicious he had ever tasted but he was too frightened to really enjoy it and had to struggle not to choke on it.

After the same thing had happened for several nights he decided to stay home and hide behind the hut so he could see who was bringing the food.

Much to his surprise the lovely maiden floated down from the painting and started preparing the food. Hu Min quickly slipped into the house, took the scroll off the wall and rolled it up. Then he fell on his knees in front of the maiden and asked for her hand in marriage. "There is no reason for us to be lonely when we can live here together happily," he said.

They were very happy together and had a beautiful son whom they loved very much. The new bride managed the household so well that the family prospered.

All this time, however, he never found out who his wife was. She would only laugh and avoid the question when he asked.

After several years had passed she became very sad and troubled and nothing he could do would cheer her up.

One day she asked Hu Min if she could see the scroll. No sooner had he gotten it unrolled than she leaped upon it and immediately became part of the painting again.

The people in the village said she was the mystery maiden from heaven and had lived out the days she was appointed to spend on earth. But Hu Min was not to be consoled. He spent the rest of his life mourning for his lost wife and every day he offered a little bowl of rice to the painting.

Tanya Lee

41

INDIA

GREEDY AND SPEEDY

In the forests of Lahore there lived two friends, a monkey named Greedy, and a rabbit named Speedy.

One day as they chatted by the roadside, along came a man carrying a cluster of bananas and a bundle of sugar cane balanced on the ends of a pole carried across his shoulders.

Said Greedy to Speedy: "If you were to sit quietly in the middle of the road as if you were hurt, the man would put the burden down and try to catch you. As he nears, you can run away. He will surely follow. And as soon as the two of you are out of sight, I will take his bananas and sugar cane and carry them off to a hiding place. Then, when the man is gone, you can return and we shall both have a great feast."

The rabbit followed the monkey's plan, and it turned out just as he had foretold. The man put his pole down and followed the rabbit, trying to catch him. The rabbit lured the man away a great distance, then raced into a hole and disappeared. Meanwhile the monkey carried off the bananas and sugar cane to the top of a banyan tree.

When the disappointed man returned and found his treasure gone, he cursed the rabbit and he cursed himself, and left. A little while later the rabbit returned and began to look high and low for his friend Greedy.

Finally he spied a pile of banana peelings under a tree. And there, on the top branch of the tree, was the monkey finishing the last banana.

"Where is my share?" asked Speedy.

"You were gone so long," replied Greedy, "and my hunger was so great, that I couldn't wait and I ate it all up."

"How could you eat it all in so short a time?" asked the rabbit.

"If you don't believe me, come up here and see for yourself."

Greedy caught Speedy by his long ears and pulled him up to the top of the tree. "Look and see!" laughed Greedy, then scampered away.

The poor rabbit was afraid to move for fear of falling down and breaking his neck. He remained in the treetop for a long time, wondering how he would ever get down safely. Many animals passed under the tree and Speedy appealed to them for help. But they could not help him. Until finally a very old rhinoceros came by and stopped to scratch his hide against the tree.

"Dear Rhinoceros," the rabbit pleaded. "You are far-famed for your strength and generosity. Please let me jump down on your back so that I may get out of this tree!"

The rhinoceros, being easily flattered, grunted assent. Speedy tumbled out of the tree and landed on the rhinoceros' neck with such force that the old rhino fell over, broke his neck, and died on the spot.

The frightened rabbit ran away and did not stop until he reached the palace of the king. There he hid himself under the golden throne, just before the king, his courtiers, and the royal guard appeared. Silken robes swished and golden swords rattled as the king ascended the throne. The rabbit became so excited that he sneezed.

"Who dares sneeze in the presence of the king?" the monarch demanded.

All the men around the throne looked at each other in terrified silence. Then another sneeze came from right under the golden throne. And Speedy was discovered.

"How dare you sneeze under my throne?" demanded the king. And he gave the order to his executioner: "Off with his head!"

Having nothing to lose now, Speedy pleaded bravely: "If Your Majesty would spare my life, I will lead your men to a large rhinoceros whose great horn, ground into powder, makes wonderful medicine."

The king laughed; then all his courtiers laughed; and the royal guard laughed with them.

"How can a rabbit lead us to a rhinoceros?" asked the king.

"If I fail to do this, you lose nothing, except having my head cut off a little later," said Speedy, feeling quite brave.

The king consented. And Speedy led the courtiers to the animal, high as a man and long as a horse, his three-toed feet up in the air, and the single horn on his nose sticking up in the air three feet high. There was the rhinoceros, just as the rabbit had promised it would be, and quite dead.

When the king was told of the find, he pardoned the rabbit and gave him a royal robe and a horse, as a reward for telling the truth. And the rabbit rode away.

Along the road he met his friend Greedy.

"Where did you get that fine robe and horse?" asked Greedy in surprise.

"The king gave them to me," said the rabbit.

"And why did the king give you all this?"

"Because I sneezed under his throne," answered Speedy.

The monkey did not stop to ask any more questions. "If a foolish rabbit can get so much from the king," thought Greedy, "what will he give to me?" He ran as fast as he could to the royal palace and hid under the golden throne.

Soon the king with his courtiers and the royal guard arrived. Silken robes swished and golden swords rattled as the king ascended the throne. Then the monkey sneezed as loud as he could.

"Who dares sneeze in the presence of the king?" the monarch demanded.

The monkey under the throne sneezed again and louder than before. At once Greedy was dragged out of his hiding place.

"How dare you sneeze under my throne?" demanded the king.

"I did it for a royal robe and a fine steed," said Greedy.

"Indeed!" thundered the king. And he gave the order to the executioner: "Take him away, and off with his head!"

Joseph Gaer

47

THE HERMIT AND THE MOUSE

In the forest of Gautama there lived a hermit who was called Mighty-in-Prayer, because whatever he prayed for came to be.

Now one day, as the good hermit sat eating his evening meal, he saw a defenseless little mouse fall at his feet from the beak of a crow. The kind hermit picked the creature up in the palm of his hand. He calmed it and warmed it and fed it with grains of wild rice. Then he found a comfortable place for the little mouse in his hermitage; and there the grateful foundling lived happily for some time.

But one day the good hermit saw a strange cat prowling about his place, chasing the poor little mouse, ready to devour him. Whereupon the hermit prayed, and the mouse instantly turned into a large fat cat. And the strange prowler ran off as fast as he could.

The hermit took good care of his cat, and all went well until one day a dog came into the neighborhood and chased the poor cat up a tree. There was the dog sitting patiently at the foot of the tree; and up there in the branches was the frightened cat, not daring to come down. The hermit prayed, and instantly the cat turned into a huge dog, so big that none of the other dogs dared harass him.

The dog lived happily with the hermit, until he wandered off into the forest one day and came upon a tiger. The dog was petrified with fright when he saw the fearful beast. But the kind hermit prayed, and instantly the dog took the form of a magnificent tiger.

The hermit still treated the tiger with the same kindness as when he was a helpless little mouse. But the mouse-turned-tiger began to think: "Only the hermit knows that I am really a mouse-turned-tiger. If I should kill him, my secret would die with him."

And so he stealthily approached the holy man one night, intent upon killing him in his sleep. But the hermit was not asleep. He saw the animal coming toward him and knew what was in the tiger's mind. And he quickly prayed: "May he turn into a mouse again!"

Instantly the great tiger turned again into a puny little mouse.

Joseph Gaer

THE MONKEY GARDENERS

In the royal gardens of Benares, a group of monkeys were allowed to roam and do as they pleased. These monkeys were great mimics. If the king came by, strolling along one of the paths, they would line up and walk behind him, just as straight and with as much dignity. If the young prince came along playing a game, they pretended they too were playing the same game. Most of all they liked to imitate the gardener. They followed him wherever he went, and whatever his task, they all imitated his motions.

A great festival was proclaimed throughout the city one day, and the gardener was eager to attend the ceremonies. But he had newly transplanted trees in the garden and did not know whom he could get to water them during the day. Then he remembered how well the monkeys imitated everything he did, and he went to their leader and said:

"His Majesty the King bestowed a great honor on you in permitting you to remain in the gardens, where you can feed on all the fruit."

"Oh, yes!" replied the monkey.

"Now there is a great festivity in the city to which I must go," the gardener went on. "To show your gratitude to His Majesty, do you think you can water the young trees while I am gone?"

"Oh, yes!" said the monkey, eagerly.

"But remember, do not waste any water," said the gardener.

"Oh, yes!" the monkey assured him.

The gardener went off to the festivities. The monkeys went happily to work and gathered together all the waterskins. They filled the containers with water and went right out to the newly planted young trees.

"Remember," commanded the leader, "do not waste any water!"

"How shall we know how much is enough, how much is too little, and how much is too much?" asked the monkeys.

"That is very simple," said he. "First you pull up the tree and look at the size of the roots. Those with long roots need much water; those with short roots need only a little water."

"How wise you are!" said all the other monkeys.

They began industriously pulling up all the newly planted trees, and watered each according to the length of its roots, just as they had been instructed.

At this point a wise man came by and noticed what the monkeys were doing. He asked them why they pulled up the trees before they watered them.

"Bcause we must water them according to the length of their roots," they explained.

And the wise man (who was the Bodisat) said:

"Like these monkeys-turned-gardeners, the ignorant and the foolish, even in their desire to do good, only succeed in doing harm."

Joseph Gaer

JAPAN

THE MAGIC LISTENING CAP

There once lived an honest old man who was kind and good, but who was so poor, he hardly had enough to eat each day. What made him sadder than not having enough to eat himself was that he could no longer bring an offering to his guardian god at the nearby shrine.

"If only I could bring even an offering of fish," he thought sadly.

Finally, one day, when his house was empty and he had nothing left to eat, he walked to the shrine of his god. He got on his knees and bowed down before him.

"I've come today to offer the only thing I have left," he said sadly. "I have only myself to offer now. Take my life if you will have it."

The old man knelt silently and waited for the god to speak.

Soon there was a faint rumbling, and the man heard a voice that seemed to come from far, far away.

"Don't worry, old man," the god said to him. "You have been honest and you have been good. From today on I shall change your fortune, and you shall suffer no longer."

Then the guardian god gave the old man a little red cap. "Take this cap, old man," he said. "It is a magic listening cap. With this

55

on your head, you will be able to hear such sounds as you have never heard before."

The old man looked up in surprise. He was old, but he heard quite well, and he had heard many, many sounds during the long years of his life.

"What do you mean?" he asked. "What new sounds are there in this world that I have not yet heard?"

The god smiled. "Have you ever really heard what the nightingale says as it flies to the plum tree in the spring? Have you ever understood what the trees whisper to one another when their leaves rustle in the wind?"

The old man shook his head. He understood.

"Thank you, dear god," he said. "I shall treasure my magic cap forever." And carrying it carefully, he hurried toward his home.

As the old man walked along, the sun grew hot, and he stopped to rest in the shade of a big tree that stood at the roadside. Suddenly, he saw two black crows fly into the tree. One came from the mountains, and the other from the sea. He could hear their noisy chatter fill the air above him. Now was the time to try his magic cap! Quickly, he put it on, and as soon as he did, he could understand everything the crows were saying.

"And how is life in the land beyond the sea?" asked the mountain crow.

"Ah, life is not easy," answered the crow of the sea. "It grows harder and harder to find food for my young ones. But tell me, do you have any interesting news from the mountains?"

"All is not well in our land either," answered the crow from the mountains. "We are worried about our friend, the camphor tree, who grows weaker and weaker, but can neither live nor die."

"Why, how can that be?" asked the crow of the sea.

"It is an interesting tale," answered the mountain crow. "About six years ago, a wealthy man in our town built a guest house in his garden. He cut down the camphor tree in order to build the house, but the roots were never dug out. The tree is not dead, but neither can it live, for each time it sends new shoots out from beneath the house, they are cut off by the gardener."

"Ah, the poor tree," said the crow of the sea sympathetically. "What will it do?"

56

"It cries and moans constantly, but alas, human beings are very stupid," said the mountain crow. "No one seems to hear it, and it has cast an evil spell on the wealthy man and made him very ill. If they don't dig up the tree and plant it where it can grow, the spell will not be broken and the man will soon die. He has been ill a long time."

The two crows sat in the tree and talked of many things, but the old man who listened below could not forget the story of the dying man and the camphor tree.

"If only I could save them both," he thought. "I am probably the only human being who knows what is making the man ill."

He got up quickly, and all the way home, he tried to think of some way in which he might save the dying man. "I could go to his home and tell him exactly what I heard," he thought. "But surely no one will believe me if I say I heard two crows talking in a tree. I must think of a clever way to be heard and believed."

As he walked along, a good idea suddenly came to him. "I shall go disguised as a fortune teller," he thought. "Then surely they will believe me."

The very next day, the old man took his little red cap, and set out for the town where the sick man lived. He walked by the front gate of this man's home, calling in a loud voice, "Fortunes! Fortunes! I tell fortunes!" Soon the gate flew open and the sick man's wife came rushing out.

"Come in, old man. Come in," she called. "Tell me how I can make my husband well. I have had doctors from near and far, but not one can tell me what to do."

The old man went inside and listened to the woman's story. "We have tried herbs and medicines from many, many lands, but nothing seems to help him," she said sadly.

Then the old man said, "Did you not build a guest house in your garden six years ago?" The wife nodded. "And hasn't your husband been ill ever since?"

"Why, yes," answered the wife, nodding. "That's right. How did you know?"

"A fortune teller knows many things," the old man answered, and then he said, "Let me sleep in your guest house tonight, and by tomorrow I shall be able to tell you how your husband can be cured."

"Yes, of course," the wife answered. "We shall do anything you say."

And so, that night after a sumptuous feast, the old man was taken to the guest house. A beautiful new quilt was laid out for him on the *tatami,* and a charcoal brazier was brought in to keep him warm.

As soon as he was quite alone, the old man put on his little red cap and sat quietly, waiting to hear the camphor tree speak. He slid open the paper doors and looked out at the sky sprinkled with glowing stars. He waited and he waited, but the night was silent and he didn't even hear the whisper of a sound. As he sat in the darkness, the old man began to wonder if the crows had been wrong.

"Perhaps there is no dying camphor tree after all," he thought. And still wearing his red cap, the old man climbed into the quilts and closed his eyes.

Suddenly, he heard a soft rustling sound, like many leaves fluttering in the wind. Then he heard a low gentle voice.

"How do you feel tonight, camphor tree?" the voice called into the silence.

Then the old man heard a hollow sound that seemed to come from beneath the floor.

"Ah, is that you, pine tree?" it asked weakly. "I do not feel well at all. I think I am about to die . . . about to die . . ." it wailed softly.

Soon, another voice whispered, "It's I, the cedar from across the path. Do you feel better tonight, camphor tree?"

And one after the other, the trees of the garden whispered gently to the camphor tree, asking how it felt. Each time, the camphor tree answered weakly, "I am dying . . . I am dying . . ."

The old man knew that if the tree died, the master of the house would also die. Early the next morning, he hurried to the bedside of the dying man. He told him about the tree and about the evil spell it had cast upon him.

"If you want to live," he said, "have the camphor tree dug up quickly, and plant it somewhere in your garden where it can grow."

The sick man nodded weakly. "I will do anything, if only I can become well and strong again."

And so, that very morning, carpenters and gardeners were called to come from the village. The carpenters tore out the floor of the guest house and found the stump of the camphor tree. Carefully, carefully, the gardeners lifted it out of the earth and then moved it into the garden where it had room to grow. The old man, wearing his red cap, watched as the tree was planted where the moss was green and moist.

"Ah, at last," he heard the camphor tree sigh. "I can reach up again to the good clean air. I can grow once more!"

As soon as the tree was transplanted, the wealthy man began to grow stronger. Before long, he felt so much better he could get up for a few hours each day. Then he was up all day long, and, finally he was completely well.

"I must thank the old fortune teller for saving my life," he said, "for if he had not come to tell me about the camphor tree, I would probably not be alive today."

And so he sent for the old man with the little red cap.

"You were far wiser than any of the doctors who came from near and far to see me," he said to the old man. Then, giving him many bags filled with gold, he said, "Take this gift, and with it my life-long thanks. And when this gold is gone, I shall see that you get more."

"Ah, you are indeed very kind," the old man said happily, and taking his gold, he set off for home.

As soon as he got home, he took some of the gold coins and went to the village market. There he bought rice cakes and sweet tangerines and the very best fish he could find. He hurried with them to his guardian god, and placed them before his shrine.

"My fortunes have indeed changed since you gave me this wonderful magic cap," the old man said. "I thank you more than I can say."

Each day after that, the old man went to the shrine, and never forgot to bring an offering of rice or wine or fish to his god. He was able to live in comfort, and never had to worry again about not having enough to eat. And, because he was not a greedy man, he put away his magic listening cap and didn't try to tell any more fortunes. Instead, he lived quietly and happily the rest of his days.

Yoshiko Uchida

THE RICE CAKE THAT ROLLED
AWAY

Long ago, in a small village in Japan, there once lived a kind old man and woman. One day, they decided they would make some rice cakes, and so the old woman made them and asked the old man to help her fill them with sweet bean paste.

It was a warm day and the sun felt good. "I think I'll take my work outside," the old man said, and he went out to the porch to work in the sun. He sat down on a little cushion, crossed his legs, and set to work. Suddenly, one of the rice cakes rolled off the plate and fell to the ground.

"*Yare, yare,*" the old man exclaimed, and he leaned over to pick it up. But just as he bent down, the rice cake began to roll away down the garden path.

"*Kora, kora!* Stop!" he shouted, but the rice cake rolled on and on.

The old man jumped off the porch, put on his wooden clogs, and ran after the rice cake.

"Where are you going in such a hurry?" he shouted as he ran.

"I'm going as far as the Ojizo-sama's shrine," the rice cake called back. It wouldn't slow down, and it wouldn't stop. It just rolled faster than ever.

The old man ran as fast as he could, but he couldn't catch up with it. Just as he got to the Ojizo-sama's shrine, he saw it disappear into a little hole. The old man peered down into the dark hole, but he couldn't see a thing. He poked his toe into the hole and found that it was much bigger than it seemed from the outside.

"Well, I guess I'll just have to crawl in after that rice cake," the old man thought to himself, and he squeezed his way into the hole. When he got inside, he found to his surprise that it was quite large and roomy.

The old man blinked and brushed the dirt from his clothes, and when he looked up he found that he was standing right in front of the stone statue of Ojizo-sama.

"Ah, forgive me, Ojizo-sama," he said, bowing low. "I did not know I would find you here. I simply came after this stupid rice cake which rolled away from my front porch."

Then the old man picked up his rice cake and broke it in two. He gave the clean half to the Ojizo-sama and kept the half covered with dirt for himself.

"Please accept my humble gift," he said, "even though it is only half a rice cake."

The statue took the rice cake, and then suddenly, in a low voice that sounded like the rumbling of the waves of the ocean, he spoke to the old man.

"Climb up on my lap," he said.

But the old man was sure he had not heard correctly. He cupped his hand behind his ear and said, "I beg your pardon, but I am old and a little deaf. What did you just say to me?"

The Ojizo-sama smiled. "I said climb up on my lap, old man," he repeated.

This time the old man knew he had heard quite clearly, but he couldn't think of climbing on the lap of the god.

"Oh no, sir. I could not possibly climb up on your lap," the old man said. "That would be most disrespectful."

But the god would not listen. "Do as I say, old man," he said.

And so the old man finally took off his clogs and climbed up on the god's lap. As soon as he did, the god spoke again. "Now, old man, get up on my shoulders!"

61

The old man shuddered. "Oh, never, never!" he said. "Why that would be a terrible thing to do."

But the Ojizo-sama insisted. "You are a stubborn old man," he said. "Do as I say."

And so the old man climbed up to the shoulders of the stone god. Then he spoke once more. "Now, old man, quickly—up on my head!"

The old man knew it was no use to refuse, so he simply did as he was told. When he had climbed on the god's head, the god handed him a fan.

"Listen carefully, old man," he said. "Very soon a group of ogres will come to gamble and drink in front of me. When they have played awhile, beat the fan and crow like a cock."

Now that seemed a very strange thing to do, but the old man listened carefully, and waited to do as he was told. Soon he heard the sound of laughter, and a crowd of ogres with horrible, ugly faces gathered in front of the statue. They rolled out dice, and took out great piles of gold which they spread on the ground. They laughed and they shouted, and they made terrible ogre-like noises that echoed and re-echoed in the emptiness of the deep hole. After a while, the old man decided it was time to do as the god had told him. He beat his fan several times, and then he crowed like a cock.

"Cockarooka-roo! Cockarooka-roo!" he shouted at the top of his voice.

When the ogres heard him, they suddenly dropped what they were doing.

"What! Is it morning already?" they shouted, and stumbling over each other, they scrambled off into the darkness, leaving behind all their gold. When the old man looked down, he saw golden coins scattered everywhere.

"Now, get down, old man," the god said, "and take all the gold the ogres left behind. It is all yours."

The old man filled two sacks with the gold the ogres had left behind. Then he bowed low to the stone god, saying, "Thank you, Ojizo-sama. You have been most generous and kind."

Then he climbed out of the hole and hurried home. When he got there, his wife was waiting patiently for him.

"Wherever have you been?" she asked. "I looked everywhere for you, but all I could find was a bowl of half-filled rice cakes!"

And so the old man told his wife how the rice cake had rolled away, and how he had followed it down to the Ojizo-sama's shrine.

The old woman's eyes grew big and round as she listened to the old man's story about the ogres and their gold. *"Mah, mah!"* she said, and she shook her head and sighed with wonder.

Then the two of them poured the gold from the sacks and counted the coins to see how much money they had. Just as they were doing this, the old woman from next door came to borrow some rice. She saw the gold spread out on the floor and rubbed her hands greedily. "My, my, where did you get all this money?" she asked. "What have you done to get so rich?"

And so the honest old man and woman told her exactly what happened.

"And you say it all began when the rice cake dropped to the ground?" she asked. "It is a strange story indeed," she said, and she hurried home to tell her husband about it. "Tomorrow I shall send my husband to the shrine to get some of the ogres' gold," she thought to herself.

Early the next morning, the greedy old man and woman next door sat on their veranda and made rice cakes. The old man waited for one to roll off the plate, but not a single one would move. Finally, he picked one up with his fingers and dropped it to the ground. The rice cake fell with a *plop,* but it stayed right where it was, and did not roll.

"What's the matter with you?" the old man said to the rice cake. "If you're not going to roll, I'll make you roll!" And jumping down from the porch, he began to kick the rice cake along the ground. He scuffled along, kicking and prodding the little rice cake, until finally he had pushed it all the way down the dusty road to the Ojizo-sama's shrine. Still the rice cake would not roll into the hole, so the old man finally pushed it in, and then climbed in after it.

Down in the hole, he found himself standing before the stone Ojizo-sama. He picked up his rice cake, ate the clean sweet bean paste from the inside, and then offered the dirty outside shell to the god.

Then, without even waiting for the god to ask him, he climbed right up on his lap. He waited a few minutes, but the god did not speak, so he climbed up on his shoulders. But still the statue remained silent, so finally the greedy old man climbed right up on his head, and waited for the ogres to come.

"Ah yes, I need the fan," the old man thought, and he leaned down and snatched it from the god's hand.

Very soon, the ogres gathered once more in front of the statue to gamble and to drink. The greedy old man watched happily as the stacks of gold grew higher and higher. Finally, when he could wait no longer, he beat the fan and crowed like a cock.

The ogres stopped, and looked around in surprise. "What? Morning already?" they shouted, and leaving their money scattered on the ground, they ran pell-mell in all directions. One little ogre was in such a hurry, his long red nose got caught in the branch of a tree.

"Help! Help! Something has grabbed my nose!" he shouted, and he stamped and kicked and looked so comical, the old man could not keep silent.

"Ha ha ha!" he burst out before he could stop himself.

And immediately, the ogres stopped. "That was the laugh of a human being," they shouted, and forgetting to run away, they began to look for the man whose voice they had just heard.

The old man sat on top of the Ojizo-sama's head and trembled with fear. "Please, don't find me," he whispered, but at last one of the ogres looked up and spotted him.

"There he is! There he is!" they shouted, and they dragged the old man from the statue. "It's not morning at all," they cried angrily. "This man tried to deceive us by crowing like a cock!" And they all pounced on him and beat him with their fists.

"Help! Help! Let me go!" the old man shouted, and at last he got away from the ogres and stumbled out of the hole.

He ran for home just as fast as he could, and didn't even stop once to look back. When he got home, his wife asked anxiously, "How much gold did you bring back? I can hardly wait to count it all."

But the old man held out his empty hands. "I was lucky to come back with my life!" he said, and he told the old woman how the ogres had found him and beat him with their fists.

"This is what comes of being so greedy," the old man said sadly, shaking his head.

And from that day on, he never tried to imitate his good neighbor again.

Yoshiko Uchida

THE ADVENTURES OF LITTLE PEACHLING

Many hundreds of years ago there lived an honest old wood-cutter and his wife. One fine morning the old man went off to the hills with his ax to gather a bundle of firewood, while his wife went down to the river to wash the clothes. There she saw a peach float-ing down the stream. She picked it up and carried it home with her, thinking to give it to her husband to eat when he came home from his labors. When the old man came down from the hills, the good wife set the peach before him. Just as he was about to eat it, the fruit split in two and a little baby boy was born into the world. The old couple took the babe and brought it up as their very own, and because he had been born in a peach, they called him Little Peachling.

Little Peachling grew up to be strong and brave, and at last one day he said to his old foster parents, "I am going to the ogres' island to carry off the riches that they have stored there. Please make me some millet dumplings for my journey."

The old folks ground the millet and made the dumplings, and Little Peachling, after bidding them an affectionate goodbye, cheer-fully set out on his travels. As he was journeying on, he met an ape. *"Kia! Kia! Kia"* the ape gibbered. "Where are you off to, Master Peachling?"

"I'm going to the ogres' island to carry off their treasure," answered Little Peachling.

"What are you carrying in your bundle?"

"I'm carrying the very best millet dumplings in all Japan."

"If you'll give me one, I will go with you," said the ape.

Little Peachling gave one of his dumplings to the ape, who took it and followed him.

When he had gone a little farther, he heard a pheasant calling, *"Ken! Ken! Ken!* Where are you off to, Master Peachling?"

Little Peachling answered as before, and the pheasant, having begged and obtained a millet dumpling, also entered his service and followed him.

A little while after, they met a dog.

"Bow! Wow! Wow! Whither away, Master Peachling?"

"I'm going to the ogres' island to carry off their treasure."

"If you will give me one of your nice millet dumplings, I will go with you," said the dog.

"With all my heart," said Little Peachling.

So he went on his way, the ape, the pheasant, and the dog following after him.

When they got to the ogres' island, the pheasant flew over the castle gate and the ape clambered over the castle wall, while Little Peachling, leading the dog, forced in the gate and entered the castle. There they had a tremendous battle with the ogres, overcame them and took their king prisoner. All the ogres did homage to Little Peachling and brought out the treasures which they had collected these many years. There were caps and coats to make their wearers invisible, jewels that governed the ebb and flow of the tide, coral, musk, emeralds, amber and tortoise shell, as well as gold and silver. All these were spread before Little Peachling by the conquered ogres.

Little Peachling shared his treasures with his companions, the ape, the pheasant, and the dog. He then set out for home laden with riches, and he maintained his foster parents in peace and plenty for the remainder of their lives.

Pearl S. Buck and Lyle Kenyon Engel

KOREA

THE MAGIC HAMMER

Thomp! thomp! thomp!

The sound of a wooden hammer on moonlit nights signals a gathering of goblins in the forests of Korea. They may meet in a secret clearing in the forest or in a remote, dimly lit cave but they are always sure they are far away from any human dwelling. It was not meant for any human to lay eyes on a feast called forth by the magic *thomp* of the goblins' hammer.

Yet there were times, even when the goblins thought they were completely hidden, that the sound of their magic hammer carried into the homes of humans. Sometimes children asleep in their beds would hear the magic *thomp* and dream about a goblins' feast in the pale moonlight.

There was even a time when a young boy happened to witness one of the fabled feasts. This is the story of how it happened.

One day, Kim Soo, a poor boy, went out to collect firewood for his parents just as he did every day. But today he had trouble finding enough wood and wandered farther into the mountains than usual. By the time it started to get dark Kim Soo realized that he was lost and decided to spend the night in a cave and wait until the morning to try and find his way home.

No sooner had Kim Soo got settled in the cave than he heard the marching of footsteps coming his way. Not knowing who might be approaching he quickly picked up his wood and hid himself in a high dark corner of the cave.

He hid himself just in time to see hundreds of little goblins rush into the cave eager to begin their merriment for the evening. The leader of the goblins pulled out his magic hammer and began to strike the floor of the cave *thomp, thomp, thomp.*

Kim Soo's eyes grew wide with excitement as he watched the forbidden sight. Each time the goblin thomped his hammer more food and wine appeared out of nowhere. The goblins ate and drank and sang and danced and gossiped about the humans and animals they had followed around all day.

"I swung on the tail of an ox as it flicked flies off its back," one goblin said with pride.

"I danced on the hand of a lovely young maiden as she drew water from the well," boasted another.

"I climbed a mountain on the back of a boy gathering firewood," claimed a third. Kim Soo held his breath thinking the last goblin might be talking about him. A chill went down his spine when he thought that a goblin might have been riding on his back all day.

Soon the goblins had drunk so much wine they all fell asleep on the floor. Then he crept out of his hiding place, grabbed the magic hammer and ran away from the cave. As soon as he was out of earshot he thomped the hammer on the ground and said, "Take me home!" In an instant he was in his own bed.

In the morning Kim Soo told his parents about his adventures and the wonderful hammer. They tried it out many times asking for a new house, clothes, food, everything they wanted and needed. Each time they struck the hammer they got what they asked for.

Of course as soon as the goblins realized their magic hammer had been stolen they set out to look for it. When they heard about a poor family who had become rich overnight, it didn't take them long to figure out that the hammer might be in that house. And sure enough one night the goblins came to Kim Soo's house and took their hammer away.

Kim Soo and his parents were very disappointed to see that their hammer was gone but in the short time they had it they had acquired all the earthly goods they needed so they were not too sad. They knew they had been blessed with good fortune and were thankful for it.

Tanya Lee

HATS TO DISAPPEAR WITH

Once upon a time in Korea there lived a bandit who was very ambitious but very unlucky. Every time he was about to steal something he would be discovered and have to make a quick getaway. Several times he had even been caught and ended up in prison.

"If only I could somehow become invisible," the bandit thought, "then all my problems would be solved." After thinking about this problem for some time he remembered that the goblins of Korea wore magic caps called Horang Gamte which had the power of making them invisible. "If only I could get my hands on one of those hats," the bandit thought and began to make plans for finding one.

He knew the goblins wore the hats when they stole food from people to take to feed the dead. So he decided he would go and wait at the graveyard until the goblins came with food. He climbed up into a tree and waited. At midnight the goblins came. Although they were invisible they made a lot of noise talking and it was still possible to see the food they carried, so the bandit began to fish for a hat wherever he saw food moving around.

At last he caught a hat on the end of his stick. As soon as the hat was off the goblin's head the bandit could see it so he had no trouble securing it. He could also see the goblin which was a very exciting thing for a human.

The goblins, however, were very frightened when one of their number lost his hat. They thought perhaps some evil spirit was after them. So they dropped all their food and ran away.

As soon as the goblins had gone, the bandit took his hat and went home.

Now he wore the hat every time he went out to steal and he became very successful. Things seemed to disappear before people's eyes and the only thing they could think of to blame it on was the goblins.

The bandit was very careful to stay away from places he thought the goblins might go in search of food. Anyway he was only interested in stealing riches and jewels. He hoped to get rich quickly and retire for he knew his luck would not hold out forever. It would only be a matter of time until the goblins started looking for their lost hat.

At first the goblins thought some evil spirit had taken their hat. But then they began to hear humans blaming them for robberies of all kinds of things they had never even thought of taking. If there was some invisible bandit out stealing things it had to be the man who took their hat.

So they began to plot how they might find the bandit and recover their hat. Perhaps they could surprise him on one of his thieving missions, grab the hat and run.

Each night the goblins would gather outside a different rich man's house hoping they might surprise the bandit. But months went by and they never saw him.

Then one day some goblins were hanging around near a jewelry merchant when the bandit came and started picking up jewels right in front of the jeweler's eyes. The jeweler couldn't figure out what was going on and thought the goblins must be after him. But the goblins could see the bandit since they had hats on too. So they simply grabbed his hat and ran away laughing about what would happen to the bandit.

All of a sudden the bandit was visible again and he was caught red-handed with the jewels and sent to jail.

When people heard the story they said the bandit deserved his bad luck because no good would ever come to a human who tried to outsmart the goblins.

Tanya Lee

GIFTS OF LOVE

In a mountain hut in Korea, an old woman lay dying. Her daughter and two sons were attending her. They were sad because they knew her time was at hand.

Once the family had been well off. But ever since the father died, the mother and children had gotten poorer and poorer. Now they barely had enough to eat.

The woman realized she was about to die and called the children to her bedside. "You know we no longer have any property. I have nothing to leave you but some tiny things to remember me by." To her daughter she gave her walking stick and a bowl made from a gourd. To the eldest son she gave an ax for chopping firewood. To the youngest son, she gave the iron cooking pot. "Now when I am gone you must go away from this lonely mountain hut and find a new life in the village. My love will follow you."

The mother died and was buried by her heartbroken children. The next day they decided they would each set out alone thinking they would fare better that way than if they tried to stay together.

The first night the daughter found a cave to sleep in. Soon after she lay down to sleep a goblin came in and said, "Come on, skeleton, come on an adventure with me."

"Where are you going?" the daughter asked.

"Your voice sounds too human," the goblin gasped. "Are you sure you're dead? Let me feel your skull."

So the daughter held out the bowl made from a gourd for the goblin to feel.

"Okay, no hair at all. But let me feel your arm."

Then the daughter held out the walking stick.

The goblin felt it and was satisfied. Thus did her mother's gifts help the daughter.

"I'm going to steal the soul of a very rich prince tonight," the goblin said gleefully.

"Oh, good, that should be an exciting adventure," the girl said.

So together they went to the palace and sneaked into the prince's bedroom whereupon the goblin stole the prince's soul and put it in a little purse. He handed the purse to the girl to take care of. Then they both ran away to hide before it got light.

The next day the whole kingdom was in mourning over the death of the prince, the king's only son.

The daughter felt very sad and set out to help the king. She begged an audience with the king and told him she thought she could restore his son to life if only she could be alone with him a few minutes.

The king had little faith in her proposal but was desperate enough to try anything so he ordered that the girl should be allowed to see the prince alone. She took the purse into his room, opened his mouth and then opened the purse into his mouth. And sure enough his soul flew back into his body and he came back to life. The king was so grateful he proposed that the young couple be married and live in the palace. And so the poor girl became a princess. She and the prince were very happy. In a few years they had a daughter and a son. When the old king died the prince became king and the poor girl became queen.

Though she was very happy she became more and more worried about the fate of her brothers about whom she had heard nothing since they parted.

She had told her kind husband the story of her life before she knew him and he resolved to help her find her brothers. He sent his messengers out to all the villages to search for the brothers. Finally one messenger came across a poor farmer in a faraway village who seemed to match the description of the queen's brother. So the messenger brought the poor farmer back to the palace with him.

The poor farmer could hardly believe his eyes when he saw the queen. He was truly amazed that his sister had managed to become a queen and was ashamed that he was only a poor farmer. But the queen was so happy to see her brother after five years she didn't care at all what he was. They were happily reunited and the brother was given a position of honor at the court.

Still the queen wondered about her other brother. Over a year had passed since she recovered her first brother and still there was no sign of the second. Finally one day a slave trader came to the court with a horde of miserable creatures. The slaves barely even looked human but the queen happened to pass by them close enough to catch the eye of one who looked particularly sick and haggard. She gasped with horror when she realized that this was her other brother. Immediately she bought the slave and nursed him back to health.

The slave could scarcely believe he had been so lucky. Not only was he now freed from slavery but he was once again reunited with his dear sister and brother. When he had recovered his strength, the king found a position for him also.

Eventually both the brothers made good marriages at the court and were blessed with children.

And all were very grateful that they were able to be together again after so long a separation.

Tanya Lee

THE TIGER AND THE HARE

Humans are not always terribly clever when it comes to out-witting tigers. When a man sees a tiger, he gets scared, starts trembling and simply loses his senses. And tigers know this.

One time there was a certain tiger who was terrorizing a small village in Korea. Every night he would come down from the mountains and take something to eat. Sometimes he would eat a chicken. Sometimes he would decide instead on a dog. And occasionally he even carried off one of the people. Everybody in the village lived in fear of the tiger. At night people bolted themselves indoors and hoped the tiger would not find a way to get into their houses.

Several times hunting parties had gone out to look for the tiger but they never had any luck finding him.

One day some of the people came up with the idea of putting food out for the tiger thinking that if it were well fed it would no longer kill to get food. But every night the tiger simply ate what the villagers had cooked for it and then went on to attack the chickens, dogs, or people.

One day someone came up with the idea of putting poison in the food they left for the tiger. So the villagers tried this. They put out a large plate of poisoned meat for the tiger. But when the tiger came that night he smelled the poison in the meat and refused to eat it.

Enraged that the villagers had tried to trick him, he carried off one of the villagers that night.

So the people no longer bothered to put food out for the tiger and lived in fear of him every night.

Now there was a wise hare living nearby who heard about the poor villagers and took pity on them. After all hares always live in fear of tigers and depend on their wits to save their lives.

So the hare came to the villagers and presented to them his plan for getting rid of the tiger. Although the villagers were doubtful that a mere hare would be able to outwit the tiger, they were willing to try anything at this point.

So the hare set about preparing his trap. He gathered up eleven smooth pebbles and prepared a fire. Then he put the pebbles in the fire and soon they began to turn red. About this time the tiger came to the village. He saw that the hare was preparing something in the fire and asked him what it was. "Oh, brother tiger, this is the most delicious new food," the hare said. "I have ten pieces and as soon as they are done I'll be glad to share them equally with you. When they have turned bright red they are most delicious. They will be even better with bean sauce. If you will tend them for a few minutes I'll go get some," the hare said running away and leaving the tiger by the fire. As soon as the hare had gone, the tiger saw that there were eleven pieces, and not ten as the hare had said. So he greedily thought that he could eat one before the hare returned and get more than his share. Thinking how clever he was, the tiger removed one of the pebbles from the fire and ate it.

The pebble burned the tiger's throat and kept burning in his stomach. He shrieked with pain and went running off to the mountains. The tiger realized too late that he had been tricked. There was nothing he could do. The pebble burned his stomach and he collapsed and died.

In the morning the hare led the villagers to the tiger's body.

The villagers could hardly believe their eyes. They were so relieved that they did not have to live in fear of the tiger any more. And they were so grateful to the clever hare that they gave him all the good food he could eat for the rest of his life.

Tanya Lee

LAOS

MISTER LAZYBONES

Under a wild fig tree there lived a man called Mister Lazybones. He had received this name from his neighbors because he was never known to have worked a day in his life. He did not even plant or hunt his food, but rather would lie all day under the fig tree and wait for the fruit to fall into his mouth. All the people scorned him and would sometimes throw rocks and dirt at him, but he was too lazy to defend himself.

One day a great wind blew some of his figs into a nearby stream. They floated downstream. The king's niece was sitting by the water and when she saw the figs float by she picked one up and ate it. It was the most delicious fruit she had ever tasted and she vowed she would marry the man to whom the figs belonged.

She told her uncle of the vow and he promised her they would try to find the man who owned the tree so she could marry. The king ordered all fig growers to bring a sample of their fruit to the court. The king's niece tasted all the figs that were brought to court, but none tasted like the one she had found in the stream. The king then inquired whether there were any fig trees in the land that had not been sampled by his niece. The people told him that the only other fig tree in the land was that of Mister Lazybones, who was too lazy to make the journey to court.

When the niece heard this she decided she would go herself and taste Mister Lazybone's figs. When she had tasted the fruit, she knew at once that this was the tree and the man she sought.

The king was very upset that his niece was going to marry such a lazy good-for-nothing, but he had given his word so he could not object. He allowed his niece to marry Mister Lazybones, but he refused to let them live at the palace and he cut off his niece's inheritance.

So they were married, and lived happily for a time. The girl was very kind to her husband and together they lived under the fig tree and enjoyed the delicious fruit.

But then one day misfortune struck. The fig tree stopped bearing fruit and the wife became very ill. Mister Lazybones was very upset because he realized he had come to love his wife very much. Never before had anyone been so kind to him or taken such good care of him.

He knew he would have to work to keep his wife alive, but he did not care because for the first time in his life he had something to work for. He tried very hard to make his wife comfortable and then set to planting new fig trees. Many new fig trees began to grow, the land prospered, and his wife got well.

When the king learned of the work that Mister Lazybones had done and of the loving care he had shown his niece, he restored his niece's inheritance and asked the couple to come and live with him at the palace.

At the palace Mister Lazybones was able to live a life of ease and comfort and once again did not have to work. He would of often think to himself, "When I was poor and lazy they called me Mister Lazybones and scorned me, but now that I am rich and lazy they call me prince and revere me." And when this thought came into his head Mister Lazybones would laugh quietly to himself at the foolishness of life.

Tanya Lee

THE LITTLE TURTLE

In a small cottage on the edge of a river there lived an old child-less couple. Theirs was a simple life: growing vegetables and catching fish from the river.

Fish were usually abundant, but one day they fished for hours without catching anything. Near sunset they found a little turtle stuck in one of their nets. They were about to throw it back, as it was of no use to them, but the little turtle cried out, "Oh, please don't throw me back. Keep me and I promise you will not regret it." The couple were amazed to hear the turtle talk. They took it back home with them and treated it as though it was their child.

The three of them lived quite happily together for nearly a year, but then one day the turtle said, "Mama, Papa, I have foreseen the future and I know that a great flood will soon ravish the land. You must build a boat so you will be saved and I must leave you and return to the water."

And so the couple heeded the words of their adopted son and began to build a boat. Soon after they had finished the building the rains began and the earth was soon flooded. It was now time for the little turtle to return to the water. He was very sad to leave but told his adopted parents not to worry and if ever they should need his help they had only to call and he would return to them. The old couple were also very sad as they watched their little turtle disappear from them into the vast floodwaters.

The couple were afloat on their boat only a few days, when a tiger swam by and asked to come aboard. The couple were frightened and did not know what to do. They called out to the little turtle to help them. No sooner had they called when their adopted son appeared from beneath the water and told them that they should let the tiger aboard as he was their friend and would repay them for their generosity. And so the tiger joined them on the boat.

The next day a snake appeared at the side of the boat and also asked to come aboard. Once again the couple called to the turtle for help. The turtle told them that they should also allow the snake to come aboard because he too was their friend and would repay them. And once again the couple followed the advice of their little turtle.

That very day a man floated by the boat and he too asked to join them. The couple let him come aboard thinking that if they could let a snake and a tiger aboard then surely they should allow a human to take shelter on their boat.

After several weeks the waters began to subside and soon the earth returned to normal. The tiger and the snake and the man all thanked the old couple for their kindness and promised to repay them if the opportunity should arise.

Nearly a year passed. The old couple returned to their land and their simple quiet life. At this time the king was traveling through the land to find out how his domain was prospering after the great flood. One night he stayed in the forest where the tiger lived. When the tiger saw the king's beautiful jewels he stole them and gave them to the old couple as payment for their kindness to him during the flood.

The couple were very glad to receive this beautiful gift. They did not know that the jewels were stolen and they put them over their hearth that they might always remember the kindness of the tiger.

One day the man whose life they had saved came to visit the couple. When he saw the jewels, he knew at once that they were those stolen from the king. He did not even ask them where they had gotten the jewels, but reported them to the court that he might collect the reward. The old couple were soon arrested and sent away to prison.

When the little turtle heard what had happened to his adopted parents he told the snake who promised he would try to help them. The snake sneaked into court and with his powerful venom blinded the king.

The king was in great pain from the snake's venom. He promised to share half his kingdom with whomever could heal him. Many great physicians came to court to try to cure the king, but none were successful.

In the meantime the snake went to the prison to visit the old couple. He brought his friends an herb which would cure the king.

And so the king was cured, and the old couple gained half a kingdom. And they never forgot the kindness of their animal friends who had more than repaid them for their kindness.

Tanya Lee

PERSIA

PRINCE AHMED AND THE FAIRY
PERIBANOU

There once was a sultan who had three sons and a niece. The eldest of the princes was called Houssain, the second Ali, the youngest Ahmed, and the princess, his niece, Nouronnibar.

The Princess Nouronnibar was the daughter of the sultan's younger brother, who had died and left her an orphan when she was very young. The sultan then took upon himself the care of his niece's education and brought her up in his palace with the three princes, thinking to marry her to some neighboring prince when she arrived at a proper age. One day he discovered that the three princes loved her passionately, and he was greatly concerned. The difficulty he foresaw was to make them agree who should have her hand in marriage. He thought that the two younger princes, in deference, should consent to give her up to their eldest brother. When he found them positively against this, he sent for all three.

"Children," he said, "since I have not been able to persuade you to choose who should marry the princess, I think it would not be amiss if each of you traveled separately into different countries, so that you will not be together, arguing with one another. As you know, I am very curious and I delight in everything that's singular. I promise my niece to the one among you who shall bring me the

91

most extraordinary rarity. For its purchase and for the expenses of traveling, I will give you each a sum of money."

As the three princes were always obedient to the sultan's will, and as each thought fortune might prove favorable to him, all consented to this arrangement. The sultan gave them the money as promised, and that very day they gave orders to their attendants to prepare for their travels, and they took their leave of the sultan. They planned to be ready to go the next morning. Accordingly, they all set out at the same gate of the city, each dressed like a merchant, attended by a trusted officer disguised as a slave. All were well mounted and equipped. They went the first day's journey together and stayed at an inn where the road branched into three other roads. At night, while at supper, all agreed to travel for a year and to meet again at the inn; whoever came first should wait for the others. Since the three had left together, it was quite possible they might all return together. The next morning, by daybreak, after they had embraced and wished one another good success, they mounted their horses and each took a different road.

Prince Houssain, the eldest brother, arrived at Bisnagar, the capital of the kingdom of that name and the residence of its king. He lodged at a khan appointed for foreign merchants, and there learned that there were four principal areas where merchants of all kinds sold their commodities and kept their shops. In the midst of this marketplace stood the king's palace. Prince Houssain went to one of those areas the next day. He was very impressed and viewed the place with admiration. It was large and divided into several streets, all vaulted and shaded from the sun, and yet very light. The shops were all of a size, and all merchants who dealt in the same kinds of goods lived in one street, as also did the handicraftsmen who kept their shops in the smaller streets.

The multitude of shops stocked with all sorts of merchandise— the finest linens of India painted in the liveliest colors with figures of beasts, trees, and flowers; silks and brocades from Persia and China; porcelains from both Japan and China; and wondrous tapestries—made him doubt his own eyes. When he came to the goldsmiths' and jewelers' shops, he was in an ecstasy to behold such prodigious quantities of wrought gold and silver, and dazzled by the luster of the pearls, diamonds, rubies, emeralds and other jewels displayed for sale.

Another thing Prince Houssain particularly admired was the great number of rose sellers who crowded the streets, for the Indians are such lovers of that flower that not one will stir without a nosegay in his hand or garland on his head. The merchants also keep roses in pots in their shops to perfume the air.

After Prince Houssain had looked over the wares in that area, street by street, his thoughts were completely filled with the riches he had seen. Since he was very tired, a merchant invited him to sit down in his shop. He had not been seated long before he saw a crier pass by with a piece of tapestry on his arm, about six feet square; the man cried this at thirty purses. The prince called to the crier and asked to see the tapestry, which seemed to him to be valued at an exorbitant price, not only for its size, but for the thinness of the stuff. When he had examined it well, he told the crier that he could not comprehend how so small and insignificant a tapestry could be valued so highly.

The crier, who took him for a merchant, replied, "If this price seems extravagant to you, your amazement will be greater when I tell you I have orders to raise it to forty purses and not to part with it under that amount."

"Certainly," answered Prince Houssain, "it must have something very extraordinary in it of which I know nothing."

"You have guessed the truth, sir," replied the crier, "and the extraordinary thing is that whoever sits on this piece of tapestry may be transported in an instant wherever he desires to be, no matter what the obstacle."

At this explanation, the Prince of the Indies, considering that the principal motive of his travel was to carry home some singular rarity, thought that he could not meet with anything which could give him more satisfaction.

"If the tapestry has the virtue you assign it," he said to the crier, "I shall not think forty purses too much, and shall make you a present besides."

"Sir," replied the crier, "I have told you the truth. It will be an easy matter to convince you. Let us strike a bargain for forty purses, on condition that I show you the experiment. But as I suppose you have not so much money about you, I will go with you to your lodgings. I will now lay the tapestry on the ground. When we have both seated ourselves, you will make the wish to be transported into your apartment at the khan. If we are not transported there, you shall be free of your bargain. As to your present, though I am paid for my trouble by the seller, I will receive it as a favor and be very much obliged to you."

The prince accepted the conditions and concluded the bargain. They both sat down on the tapestry, and as soon as the prince made his wish, lo and behold, he presently found himself and the crier at his lodgings. As he wanted no further proof of the tapestry's virtue, he counted out forty purses of gold for the crier and gave him twenty pieces for himself.

In this manner Prince Houssain became the possessor of the tapestry. He was overjoyed that in the short time he had been in Bisnagar he had already found so rare a piece, which he was positive would gain him the hand of Nouronnibar. In short, he looked upon it as impossible for his younger brothers to meet with anything to be compared with what he had found. It was in his power, by sitting on his tapestry, to be at the place of meeting that very day, but since he would be obliged to wait there for his brothers, as they had agreed, and as he was curious to see the King of Bisnagar and his court and to inform himself of the strength, laws, customs, and religion of the kingdom, he chose to spend some months there and satisfy his curiosity.

Time passed, and although Prince Houssain might have stayed longer at the court of Bisnagar, he was so eager to be nearer the princess that he spread the tapestry, he and the officer he had brought with him sat upon it, and, as soon as he had made his wish, they were transported to the inn where he and his brothers were to meet.

Prince Ali, the second brother, who wanted to travel into Persia, took the road that led there, joined a caravan and, after four days' travel, arrived in Shiraz, which was the capital of the kingdom. Here he passed for a jeweler. The next morning, he dressed himself and took a walk into the bazaar of Shiraz.

Among all the criers who passed up and down with their wares he was surprised to see one who held in his hand an ivory telescope about a foot in length and the thickness of a man's thumb, crying it at thirty purses. At first he thought the crier mad. To inform himself further, he walked over to a merchant standing at his shop door and said, "Pray, sir, is not that man mad? If he is not, I am very much deceived."

"Indeed, sir," the merchant answered, "he was in his right senses only yesterday; I can assure you he is one of the ablest criers we have, and the most employed of any when something valuable is to be sold. If he cries the ivory telescope at thirty purses, it must be worth as much or more. He will come by here presently, and we will call him and you shall be satisfied. In the meantime, sit down on my sofa and rest yourself."

Prince Ali accepted the merchant's kind offer, and presently the crier passed by. The merchant called him by name and, pointing to the prince, said, "Tell that gentleman what you mean by crying that small telescope at thirty purses. I should be very much amazed myself, if I did not know you."

The crier, addressing himself to Prince Ali, said, "Sir, you are not the only person who takes me for a madman because of this telescope. You shall judge for yourself when I have told you its property. First, sir," pursued the crier, presenting the ivory pipe to the prince, "observe that this pipe is furnished with a glass at both ends and consider that by looking through one of them you can see whatever object you wish to behold."

"I am ready to make reparation if this is truly so," the prince said, and holding the ivory tube in his hand, he went on, "Show me at which end I must look that I may be satisfied."

The crier showed him, and the prince looked through, wishing at the same time to see his father—whom he immediately beheld in perfect health, sitting on his throne in the midst of his council. Then, as there was nothing in the world so dear to him, after the sultan, as the Princess Nouronnibar, he wished to see her, and there she was in her dressing room laughing and in a pleasant humor, with her women all about her. Prince Ali wanted no future proof that this telescope was the most valuable thing in world; he was sure that he would never again meet with such a rarity. He therefore took the crier with him to the khan where he lodged, and paid him the money and received the magic telescope.

95

Prince Ali was overjoyed at his bargain and persuaded himself that, as his brothers would not be able to find anything so rare and admirable, the Princess Nouronnibar would be his. As soon as the caravan was ready to return, the prince joined it and arrived at the inn happily without accident or trouble other than the length of the journey and the fatigue of traveling. There he found Prince Houssain, and both waited for Prince Ahmed.

Prince Ahmed took the road to Samarkand, and when he got there he heard a crier, who had an artificial apple in his hand, cry it at thirty-five purses. He stopped the crier and said to him, "Let me see that apple, and tell me what virtues and extraordinary properties it has to be valued at so high a price."

"Sir," said the crier, placing the apple in his hand, "if you look at the outside of this apple it appears worthless, but if you consider its properties and the great use and benefit it is to mankind, you will say thirty-five purses is no price at all, and that he who possesses it is master of a great treasure. In short, it cures all sick persons of the most mortal diseases, and if the patient is dying it will cause him to recover immediately and restore him to perfect health. This is accomplished merely by the patient's smelling the apple."

"If I may believe you," replied Prince Ahmed, "the virtues of this apple are wonderful indeed. First you will have to show me that this is so."

"Sir," replied the crier, "the apple is known and believed in by the whole city of Samarkand. Ask all these merchants you see here, and listen to what they say. Several will tell you that they would not be alive this day if they had not made use of this excellent remedy. It is the fruit of the study and experiments of a celebrated philosopher of this city. All his lifetime he applied himself to the study and knowledge of the virtues of plants and minerals and at last produced this apple, by which he performed many surprising cures. But he himself died suddenly, before he could apply his own remedy. He left his wife and many young children behind him. They are in want, and she will sell it to provide for her children."

Meanwhile a great many persons gathered around them and confirmed what he said. One said he had a friend who was now dangerously ill and whose life was despaired of, and that this was a favorable opportunity to allow Prince Ahmed to perform the experiment. Upon hearing this, Prince Ahmed told the crier he would give him forty purses if he cured the sick person.

The crier said to Prince Ahmed, "Come, sir, let us go and make the experiment, and the apple shall be yours. I can assure you that it will always have the desired effect."

In short, the experiment succeeded, and the prince, after he had counted out to the crier forty purses, received the apple. He waited patiently for the first caravan that would return to the Indies and arrived in perfect health at the inn where the Princes Houssain and Ali waited for him.

When the princes met they showed each other their treasures. What was their consternation when they saw through the glass that the princess was dying. They sat down on the carpet at once, wishing themselves with her, and were there in a moment.

As soon as Prince Ahmed was in Nouronnibar's chamber he arose from the tapestry, as did the other two princes, and went to the bedside, where they put the apple under her nose. Some moments after, the princess opened her eyes and turned her head from one side to another, looking at the persons who stood about her. She then sat up in bed and asked to be dressed, just as if she had awakened out of a sound sleep. Her women told her joyfully that she had the three princes to thank for the sudden recovery of her health, particularly Prince Ahmed. She immediately expressed her joy at seeing them and thanked all together, and afterward Prince Ahmed in particular.

While the princess was dressing, the princes went to throw themselves at their father's feet and pay their respects. When they came before him they found that the princess' chief eunuch had already informed the sultan of their arrival and by what means the princess had been cured. The sultan received and embraced them with the greatest joy, both for their return and for the recovery of the princess, whom he loved as well as if she had been his own daughter. After the usual ceremonies and compliments the princes each presented his rarity. Prince Houssain his tapestry, Prince Ali his ivory telescope, and Prince Ahmed his artificial apple. They put the decision into the sultan's hands and begged him to pronounce their fate—to which of them he would give the Princess Nouronni-bar for a wife, according to his promise.

The Sultan of the Indies, having heard all that the princes could tell about their rarities and how the princess had been saved, remained silent for some time, thinking what answer he would make.

At last he broke his silence and said, "I would give her to one of you children with a great deal of pleasure if I could do so with justice; but consider whether I can or not. It is true, Prince Ahmed, the princess is obliged to your artificial apple for her cure. But could you have cured her if you had not known by Prince Ali's telescope the danger she was in, and if Prince Houssain's tapestry had not brought you here so soon.

"Your telescope, Prince Ali, informed you and your brothers that you were likely to lose the princess and to the telescope all of you must owe a great obligation. You must also grant that your knowledge would have been of no service without the artificial apple and the tapestry.

"And lastly, Prince Houssain, the princess would be very ungrateful if she did not acknowledge the service of your tapestry, which was so necessary for her cure. But consider, it would have been of little use if you had not been acquainted with the princess' illness by means of Prince Ali's glass, and if Prince Ahmed had not applied his artificial apple. Therefore, as neither tapestry, ivory telescope, nor artificial apple has the least preference one before the other, but as, on the contrary, there is a perfect equality, I cannot grant the princess to any one of you, and the only fruit you have reaped from your travels is the glory of having equally contributed to restore her health.

"If all this be true," added the sultan, "you see that I must have recourse to other means to determine the choice I ought to make among you. Therefore, go, each of you, get bow and arrow and meet me on the great plain where they exercise the horses. I now declare that I will give the Princess Nouronnibar to the one that shoots the farthest."

The three princes had nothing to say against the decision of the sultan. When they left his presence, each provided himself with a bow and arrow and went to the place appointed for the event, followed by a great multitude of people.

As soon as the sultan arrived, Prince Houssain, as the eldest, took his bow and arrow and shot first; Prince Ali shot next, and much beyond his brother's shot. Prince Ahmed drew bow last of all, but it so happened that nobody could see where his arrow fell. It was not to be found far or near. And though it was believed that he had shot the farthest and that he therefore deserved the Princess Nouronnibar, this could not be proved. The sultan judged in favor of Prince Ali and gave orders for preparations to be made for the wedding, which was celebrated a few days after with great magnificence.

Prince Houssain would not honor the feast with his presence. His grief was so deep that he left the court and renounced all right of succession to the crown to turn hermit. Prince Ahmed, too, did not come to the wedding, any more than his brother Houssain; but, unlike his brother, he did not renounce the world. Determined to discover what had become of his arrow, he stole away from his attendants and resolved to search for it. He went first to the place where Prince Houssain's and Prince Ali's arrows had been gathered up, and, going straightforward from there, looking carefully on both sides, he went so far that at last he began to think his labor was all in vain. Yet he could not help going forward, until he came to some steep craggy rocks situated in a barren country about four leagues distant from where he had set out.

Close by these rocks he perceived an arrow. He picked it up and looked at it intently. He was greatly astonished to find it was the same one he had shot away. "Certainly," he said to himself, "neither I nor any man living could shoot an arrow so far," and finding that it lay flat, not thrust into the ground, he judged that it had rebounded against the rock. "There must be some mystery in this," he thought, "and it may be advantageous to me. Perhaps fortune brought it here to make amends for losing what I thought to be my greatest happiness."

The rocks were full of caves, some of which were deep. The prince entered one, and, in looking about, his eyes fell on an iron door which seemed to have no lock. As he pushed against it, the door opened, showing an easy descent, down which he walked with his arrow in his hand. At first he walked in shadowy dimness, but presently a light shone ahead of him, and, entering into a large, spacious place about fifty or sixty paces distant, he perceived there a magnificent palace. At the same time a lady of majestic air advanced toward him, attended by a large group of women, each so finely dressed and beautiful that it was difficult to distinguish which was the mistress.

As soon as Prince Ahmed saw the lady he made all haste to pay his respects. The lady, on her part, seeing him coming, addressed him first, saying, "Come nearer, Prince Ahmed. You are welcome."

It was no small surprise to the prince to hear his name spoken in a place he had never even heard of—and so near his father's capital. He did not understand how he could be known to a lady who was a stranger to him. He returned the lady's compliment by throwing himself ₁at her feet, and upon rising again he said, "Madam, a thousand thanks for your welcome. But may I dare to ask by what chance you know me, and how it is that you should be so completely a stranger to me?"

. "Prince," said the lady, "let us go into the hall. There I will answer your questions."

The lady then led Prince Ahmed into the hall. Then she sat down on a sofa, and, when the prince by her entreaty had done the same, she said, "You are undoubtedly aware that your religion teaches you to believe that the world is inhabited by genii as well as by men. I am the daughter of one of the most powerful and distinguished genii and my name is Peribanou. You seemed to me worthy of a happier fate than that of marrying the Princess Nouronnibar. I was present when you drew your arrow, and I foresaw it would not go beyond Prince Houssain's. I took it in the air and made it strike against the rocks near which you found it. Now I tell you that it lies in your power to use this favorable opportunity to make yourself happy."

As the fairy Peribanou pronounced these last words her tone changed, and she looked tenderly at Prince Ahmed, a modest blush on her cheeks. It was no hard matter for the prince to comprehend what happiness she meant. He presently considered that the Princess Nouronnibar could never be his, and that the fairy Peribanou excelled her infinitely in beauty, agreeableness, wit, and as much as he could conjecture by the magnificence of the palace, immense riches. He blessed the moment that he had thought of seeking his arrow a second time; and yielding to his love he replied, "Madam, should I all my life have the happiness of being your slave and the admirer of the many charms which ravish my soul, I should think myself the most blessed of men. Pardon the boldness which inspires me to ask this favor, and do not refuse to admit into your court a prince who is entirely devoted to you."

"Prince," answered the fairy, "will you not pledge your faith to me when I pledge mine to you?"

"Yes, madam," replied the prince in an ecstasy of joy. "What can I do better and with greater pleasure? Yes, my Sultana, my Queen, I give you my heart without the least reserve."

"Then," answered the fairy, "you shall be my husband and I your wife. But as I suppose that you have eaten nothing today," she continued, "a slight repast shall be served you while preparations are made for our wedding feast tonight, and then I will show you the apartments of my palace."

Some of the fairy's attendants now left the hall and returned presently with some excellent meats and wines. When Prince Ahmed had eaten, the fairy Peribanou took him through all the apartments, where he saw diamonds, rubies, emeralds and other fine jewels, intermixed with pearls, agate, jasper, porphyry, and the most precious marbles. The prince said that he could not have imagined such beauty.

"Prince," said the fairy, "if you admire my palace so much, which, indeed, is very beautiful, what would you say to the palaces of the chief of our genii, which are much more beautiful, spacious and magnificent? I could also charm you with my gardens, but we will let that wait until another time. Night draws near, and it is time to go to supper."

The next hall into which the fairy led the prince, where the cloth was laid for the feast, was the last apartment the prince had not seen. As he entered it he admired the infinite number of sconces of wax candles perfumed with amber; this multitude of lights, instead of giving the appearance of confusion, was placed with so just a symmetry as to form an agreeable sight. A large side table was set out with every variety of gold plate, so finely wrought that the workmanship was even more valuable than the gold. Several choruses of beautiful women richly dressed began a concert, accompanied by the most harmonious instruments. When they sat down at the table the fairy Peribanou took care to help Prince Ahmed to the most delicate meats, which the prince found to be so exquisitely good that he commended them with exaggeration, and also said that the entertainment far surpassed any devised by man. He found also the same excellence in the wines, which neither he nor the fairy tasted until the dessert, consisting of the choicest sweetmeats and fruits, was served. The wedding feast was continued the next day, and the days following the celebration were festive indeed.

At the end of six months Prince Ahmed, who still loved and honored the sultan, conceived a great desire to know how he was, but that desire could not be satisfied without a visit. He told the fairy of it and asked her leave.

"Prince," said she, "go when you please. But do not take it amiss that I give you some advice on how you shall conduct yourself. First, it is not proper for you to tell your father of our marriage, nor of my rank nor of this place. Beg him to be satisfied in knowing you are happy and to desire no more. Let him know that the sole purpose of your visit is to make him easy and inform him that you are well."

She appointed twenty gentlemen, well mounted and equipped, to attend him. When all was ready, Prince Ahmed took his leave of the fairy, embracing her and renewing his promise to return soon. Then his horse, which was most finely caparisoned and as beautiful a creature as any in the Sultan of the Indies' stables, was led to him, and he mounted him with an extraordinary grace. After he had bid the fairy a last fond adieu he set forth on his journey.

Since it was not far to his father's capital, Prince Ahmed soon arrived. The people were glad to see him again, and receiving him with acclamation, they followed him in crowds to the sultan's apartment. The sultan received him with great joy, complaining at the same time with fatherly tenderness of the affliction his long absence had been.

The prince told the story of his adventures without speaking of the fairy, in accordance with the promise he had made her, and ended, "The only favor I ask of Your Majesty is to allow me to come often and pay you my respects and see how you are."

"Son," answered the Sultan of the Indies, "I cannot refuse what you ask me, but I would much rather you resolved to stay with me. At least tell me where I may send word to you if you should fail to come, or when I think your presence necessary."

"Sire," replied Prince Ahmed, "what Your Majesty asks of me is part of the mystery of which I spoke. I beg you to allow me to remain silent on this subject, for I shall come so frequently that I am afraid that I shall sooner be thought troublesome than be accused of negligence of my duty."

The Sultan of the Indies pressed Prince Ahmed no more but said to him, "Son, I penetrate no further into your secrets, but grant you your liberty. You can do me no greater pleasure than to come often and by your presence restore to me the joy I have not felt this long time. You shall always be welcome."

Prince Ahmed stayed but three days at his father's court; and on the fourth day he returned to the fairy Peribanou.

A month after Prince Ahmed's return from the visit to his father, the fairy Peribanou said to him, "Prince, tell me, have you forgotten the sultan, your father? Do you not remember the promise you made to go and see him often? For my part, I have not forgotten what you told me at your return, and so I put you in mind of it."

Prince Ahmed went the next morning with an even finer retinue than before, and he himself more magnificently mounted, equipped and dressed than before, and was received by the sultan with the same joy and satisfaction. For several months he continued his visits, and always with a richer and finer equipage. At last some viziers, the sultan's favored counselors, who judged Prince Ahmed's grandeur and power by the figure he cut, made the sultan jealous of his son, saying it was to be feared he might inveigle himself into the people's favor and dethrone the sultan.

The Sultan of the Indies was far from thinking that Prince Ahmed could be capable of so terrible a plan. He said to them, "You are mistaken. My son loves me, and I am certain of his tenderness and fidelity."

But the counselors went on abusing Prince Ahmed until the sultan said, "I don't think my son Ahmed is as wicked as you would have me believe. However, I am obliged to you for your good advice, and I don't dispute that it comes from good intentions."

The Sultan of the Indies resolved to have Prince Ahmed watched, unknown to his grand vizier. So he sent for a female magician, who came by a back door into his apartment. "Go immediately," he said, "and follow my son when he leaves here. Watch him well, find out where he lives, and bring me word."

The magician left the sultan and, knowing the place where Prince Ahmed had found his arrow, went there immediately and hid herself near the rocks.

The next morning Prince Ahmed set out from his father's palace by daybreak.

The magician, seeing him coming, followed him with her eyes. Suddenly she lost sight of him and his attendants. The rocks were so steep and craggy that they should have been an insurmountable barrier, so that the magician judged there were but two explanations for the prince's disappearance—either he must have vanished into a cavern or visited the abode of a genie or fairy. She then came out of the place where she was hidden and went to the farther end, looking carefully about on all sides. Notwithstanding all her diligence, she could find no opening, not so much as the iron gate which Prince Ahmed had discovered, for this gate could be seen and opened only by those whose presence was agreeable to the fairy Peribanou. The magician, seeing that it was useless to search any further, had to be satisfied with the discovery she had made, and she returned to give the sultan an account.

The sultan was well pleased with the magician's conduct and said to her, "Do as you think fit. I'll wait patiently for more information." And to encourage her he made her a present of a diamond of great value.

Since Prince Ahmed had obtained the fairy Peribanou's leave to go to the Sultan of the Indies' court once a month, he never failed to do so. A day before one of these visits, the magician went again to the foot of the rock. There she waited all night.

The next morning Prince Ahmed went out as usual by the iron gate, with the same attendants as before, and passed by the magician. He saw her lying with her head against the rock and moaning as if she were in great pain. Pitying her, he turned his horse about and went to her and asked her what was the matter.

The artful sorceress looked at the prince in a pitiful manner, without lifting her head, and answered in broken words and sighs, as if she could hardly catch her breath, that she had been bound for the capital city, but on the way there she had been taken with so violent a fever that her strength had failed her and she was forced to lie down where he saw her, far from any habitation and without any hope of assistance.

"Good woman," replied Prince Ahmed, "you are not so far from help as you imagine. I am ready to assist you and take you where you will find a speedy cure. Rise and let one of my men take you on his horse."

At these words the magician, who had pretended sickness only to know where the prince lived and what he did, could not refuse his charitable offer. One of the prince's attendants, alighting from his horse, helped her up, set her behind him and followed the prince, who turned back to the iron gate. When he came into the outer court, without dismounting he sent one of his men to tell the fairy he wanted to speak with her.

The fairy Peribanou came with all haste, wondering what had made Prince Ahmed return so soon. The prince, giving her no time to ask him the reason, said, "Princess, I desire you to have compassion on this good woman," pointing to the magician, who was being held up by two of his retinue. "I found her in this condition and promised her aid. Please, out of your own goodness, do not abandon her."

The fairy Peribanou, who had her eyes fixed upon the false invalid all the time that the prince was talking to her, ordered two of her women to carry the old woman into the palace and take care of her.

While the two women executed the fairy's commands, she went up to Prince Ahmed and, whispering to him, said, "Prince, this woman is not so sick as she pretends to be, and I believe she is an imposter who will be the cause of great trouble to you. But don't be concerned. I will deliver you from all the snares that will be laid for you. Go and continue your journey."

This discourse of the fairy's did not in the least frighten Prince

Ahmed. "My Princess," he said, "I do not remember that I ever did anybody an injury and I do not believe anybody can have a thought of doing me one."

In the meantime the two women carried the magician into a richly furnished apartment. First they sat her down upon a sofa, with her back supported on a cushion of gold brocade, while they made up a bed on the same sofa, the quilt of which was finely embroidered with silk, the sheets of the finest linen, and the coverlet cloth of gold. When they had put her into bed—for the old sorceress pretended that her fever was so violent she could not help herself in the least—one of the women went out and soon returned holding in her hands a china cup full of a certain liquor, which she presented to the magician.

"Drink this," she said. "It is the water of the fountain of lions and a sovereign remedy against all fevers. You will feel the effect of it in less than an hour's time."

The magician took the cup after a great deal of entreaty and, bending her head back, swallowed down the liquor. When she was bedded down again the two women covered her. "Lie quiet," said the one who had brought her the china cup, "and get a little sleep if you can. We'll leave you and hope to find you perfectly cured when we come again an hour hence."

The two women returned in an hour and found the magician dressed and sitting up on the sofa. "O admirable potion!" she cried. "It has wrought its cure much sooner than you told me it would, and I shall be able to continue my journey."

The two women, who were fairies like their mistress, walked before her and conducted her through several apartments, all nobler than that wherein she lay, and then into a large hall, the most richly and magnificently furnished in the palace.

Peribanou sat in this hall on a throne of massive gold enriched with diamonds, rubies, and pearls of an extraordinary size, and attended on each hand by a great number of beautiful fairies, all richly clothed. At the sight of such majesty the magician was not only dazzled but so amazed that, after she had prostrated herself before the throne, she could not open her lips to thank the fairy as she intended. Peribanou saved her the trouble and said to her. "Good woman, I am glad I have had an opportunity to help you and to see that you are able to pursue your journey. I will not detain you—perhaps you may not be displeased to see my palace. Follow my women and they will show it to you."

Then the magician went back and related to the Sultan of the Indies all that had happened; she told him how very rich Prince Ahmed was since his marriage to the fairy, richer than all the kings in the world, and how there was danger that he might come and take the throne from his father.

Though the Sultan of the Indies felt that Prince Ahmed's natural disposition was good, yet he could not help being concerned at the words of the old sorceress. When she was taking her leave, he said, "I thank you for the pains you have taken and your good advice. I will remember it, and I shall deliberate upon it in council."

The spiteful counselors advised that the prince should be killed, but the magician disagreed. "Make him give you all kinds of wonderful things with the fairy's help, until she tires of him and sends him away. For example, every time Your Majesty goes into the field, you have a great expense, not only in pavilions and tents for your army, but likewise in mules and camels to carry their baggage. Now, you must ask him to use his influence with the fairy to secure you a tent which could be carried in a man's hand and yet be so large as to shelter your whole army against bad weather."

When the magician had finished her speech, the sultan asked his counselors if they had anything better to propose and, finding them all silent, determined to follow the magician's advice.

Next day the sultan did as the magician had advised him. Prince Ahmed had never expected that his father would ask a thing so difficult, in fact, impossible. Though he did not know how great the power of genii and fairies was, he doubted whether it extended so far as to include such a tent as his father desired.

At last he replied, "I will not fail to ask my wife the favor Your Majesty desires, but I will not promise you to obtain it. If I should not have the honor to come again to pay you my respects, that shall be the sign that I have not had success. But beforehand I desire you to forgive me, and consider that you yourself have placed me in this position."

"Son," replied the Sultan of the Indies, "I should be very sorry if what I ask of you should cause me the displeasure of never seeing you again. I think you do not know the power a husband has over a wife, and yours would show that her love for you was very indifferent if she, with her fairy's power, should refuse you so trifling a request."

The prince went back, very sad and fearful of offending the fairy. She kept pressing him to tell her what was the matter, and at last he said, "Madam, you may have observed that hitherto I have been content with your love and have never asked you any other favor. Consider, then, I beg you, that it is not I, but the sultan, my father, who indiscreetly asks of you a pavilion large enough to shelter him, his court, and his army from the violence of the weather, and one which a man may carry in his hand. Please remember it is my father who asks this favor."

"Prince," replied the fairy, smiling, "I am sorry that so small a matter should disturb you and make you uneasy."

Then the fairy sent for her treasurer, to whom she said, "Nourgihan, bring me the largest pavilion in my treasury."

Nourgihan returned presently with the pavilion, which she could not only hold in her hand, but in the palm of her hand when she shut her fingers. She presented it to her mistress, who gave it to Prince Ahmed.

When Prince Ahmed saw the pavilion which the fairy called the largest in her treasury, he fancied she was jesting with him. At the surprised look on his face, Peribanou burst out laughing.

"What, Prince?" she cried. "Do you think I jest with you? You will see presently that I am in earnest. Nourgihan," she said to her treasurer, taking the tent out of Prince Ahmed's hands, "go and set it up, that the prince may judge whether it will be large enough for the sultan."

The treasurer went immediately with it out of the palace and carried it a great way off, and when she had set it up, one end reached to the very palace. The prince found it large enough to shelter two armies greater than that of the sultan's.

"I ask my princess a thousand pardons for my incredulity," he said to Peribanou. "After what I have seen I believe there is nothing impossible to you."

"You see," said the fairy, "that the pavilion is larger than your

108

father may have occasion for. It has one unusual property: it can become larger or smaller, according to the army it is to cover."

The treasurer took down the tent again and brought it to the prince, who took it, mounted his horse, and went with his retinue to the sultan's palace.

The sultan, who had not really believed there could be such a pavilion, was greatly surprised at the prince's success. He took the tent, and after he had examined it his amazement was so great that he could not recover his composure. When the tent was set up on the great plain, he found it large enough to shelter an army twice as large as he could bring into the field.

Yet he was not satisfied. "Son," he said, "I have already told you how much I am obliged to you for the gift of the tent. I look upon it as the most valuable thing in all my treasury. Still, you must do one thing more for me. I am informed that the fairy, your wife, makes use of a certain water called the water of the fountain of lions, which cures all sorts of fevers, even the most dangerous. As I am sure my health is dear to you, I don't doubt you will ask her for a bottle of that water for me to use when I have the need. Do this for me and thereby complete the duty of a good son toward a tender father."

The prince returned and told the fairy what his father had said. "There is a great deal of wickedness in this dangerous demand, as you will understand by what I tell you," she answered. "The fountain of lions is in the middle of a court of a great castle, the entrance of which is guarded by four fierce lions. Two of them sleep while the other two stand watch. But don't let that frighten you. I will give you means to pass by them without any danger."

The fairy Peribanou was at that time very hard at work with several balls of thread by her side. She took one up and, presenting it to Prince Ahmed, she said, "First, take this—I'll tell you its use presently. Second, you must have two horses. One you must ride yourself, and the other you must lead. It must be loaded with a sheep that must be killed today and cut into four quarters. Third, I will give you a bottle in which to bring back the water. Set out early tomorrow morning, and when you have passed the iron gate throw the ball of thread before you. It will roll until it comes to the gates of the castle. Follow it, and when it stops, as the gates open you will see the four lions. The two that are awake will by their roaring wake the other two, but don't be frightened. Just throw each of them a quarter of mutton. Then clap spurs to your horse and ride to the fountain. Fill your bottle without alighting and return the same way. The lions will be so busy eating that they will let you pass."

Prince Ahmed set out the next morning at the time appointed by the fairy and followed her directions exactly. When he arrived at the gates of the castle he distributed the quarters of mutton among the four lions, and passing bravely through their midst, got to the fountain, filled his bottle, and returned as safe and sound as he went. When he had gone a little distance from the castle gates he turned and saw two of the lions coming after him. He drew his saber and prepared himself for defense. But as he went forward he saw one turn off the road at some distance. The lion showed by gesture of his head and tail that he did not come to do him any harm, but only to go before him; and the other stayed behind him to guard his rear. He put his sword again into the scabbard. Guarded in this manner, he arrived at the capital of the Indies, but the lions never left him until they had conducted him to the gates of the sultan's palace. Then they returned the same way they came, frightening all who saw them, even though they proceeded in a gentle manner and showed no fierceness whatsoever.

Many officers came to attend the prince while he dismounted from his horse, and they conducted him into the sultan's apartments. The sultan was at that time surrounded by his counselors. The prince approached the throne, laid the bottle at the sultan's feet and kissed the rich tapestry that covered his footstool. "I have brought you, sir, the healthful water which Your Majesty desired," he said. "At the same time I wish you such extraordinary health as never to have occasion to make use of it."

After the prince had ended his compliment the sultan placed him on his right hand and said to him, "Son, I am very much obliged to you for this valuable present, and also for the great danger you have exposed yourself to on my account. I have been informed of this by a magician who knows the fountain of lions.

But do me the pleasure," he continued, "to inform me by what incredible power you have been able to deliver the healing water."

"Sir," replied Prince Ahmed, "I have no share in the compliment Your Majesty is pleased to make me. All the honor is due to the fairy, my wife, whose good advice I followed."

Then he informed the sultan what those directions were, and by relating his expedition let him know how well he had conducted himself. When he had finished, the sultan, who showed outwardly all the demonstrations of great joy, secretly became more jealous and retired into an inner apartment, where he sent for the magician.

"Son," said the sultan the following day, "I have one thing more to ask of you, after which I shall expect nothing more from your obedience. This request is to bring me a man not above a foot and a half high, but whose beard is thirty feet long and who carries a bar of iron on his shoulders of five hundredweights, which he uses as a quarterstaff."

Prince Ahmed did not believe that there was such a man in the world as his father described. The sultan persisted in his demand and told him the fairy could do much more incredible things. The next day the prince returned to his dear Peribanou, to whom he told his father's new command, which seemed to him even more impossible than the first two.

"For," he added, "I cannot imagine that there exists such a man in the world. I think my father is just testing me to see if I am so silly as to try to find him, or perhaps he wishes my ruin. How can he suppose that I should conquer a man so well armed, though small? What arms can I use to bend him to my will? If there are any means, I beg you will tell them and let me come off with honor this time."

"Fear not, my Prince," the fairy replied. "You ran a risk in fetching the water of the fountain of lions for your father, but there is no danger in finding this man, who is my brother Schaibar. He is different from me, though we both had the same father, and he is of so violent a nature that nothing can prevent his showing his resentment for a slight offense. Yet, on the other hand, he is so good as to oblige all in whatever they desire. He is exactly as your father described him, and I'll send for him. But be sure to

111

prepare yourself against being frightened at his extraordinary figure when you see him."

"What, my Queen?" Prince Ahmed replied. "Do you say Schaibar is your brother? Let him be ugly or deformed, I shall never be frightened at the sight of him. As our brother, I shall honor and love him."

The fairy ordered a gold chafing dish to be set with a fire in it under the porch of her palace, with a box of the same metal, out of which she took a perfume and threw it into the fire. There arose a thick cloud of smoke.

Some moments after, the fairy said to Prince Ahmed, "See, here comes my brother."

The prince saw Schaibar coming gravely with his heavy bar on his shoulder, his long beard which he held up before him, and a pair of thick mustaches, which were tucked behind his ears and almost covered his face. His eyes were very small and set deep in his head, on which he wore a grenadier's cap. Besides all this, he was very humpbacked. If Prince Ahmed had not known that Schaibar was Peribanou's brother, he would not have been able to look at him without fear, but as it was he stood beside his wife without the least concern.

Schaibar, as he came forward, looked at the prince earnestly enough to have chilled his blood in his veins, and asked Peribanou who the man was. She replied, "He is my husband, brother. His name is Ahmed and he is son to the Sultan of the Indies. The reason why I did not invite you to my wedding was that I was unwilling to divert you from an expedition in which you were engaged and from which I heard with pleasure you returned victorious. I took the liberty now to call for you."

At these words Schaibar, looking on Prince Ahmed favorably, said, "Is there any way, sister, in which I can serve him? It is enough for me that he is your husband to engage me to do whatever he desires."

"The sultan, his father," Peribanou replied, "has a curiosity to see you, and I desire that my husband be your guide to the sultan's court."

"He needs but lead the way. I will follow him."

"Brother," Peribanou replied, "it is too late to go today. Therefore stay until tomorrow morning, and in the meantime I'll inform you of all that has passed between the Sultan of the Indies and Prince Ahmed since our marriage."

The next morning, Schaibar and Prince Ahmed set out for the sultan's court. When they arrived at the gates of the capital and the people saw Schaibar, they ran and hid themselves. Some shut up their shops and locked themselves in their houses, while others fled, communicating their fear to all they met. These stayed not to look behind them but ran too. Schaibar and Prince Ahmed found the streets all desolate until they came to the palace, where the porters, instead of keeping the gates, ran away, too. The prince and Schaibar thus advanced without any obstacle to the council hall, where the sultan was seated on his throne giving audience. Here likewise, the ushers, at the approach of Schaibar, abandoned their posts and gave the two free admittance.

Schaibar went boldly and fiercely up to the throne without waiting to be presented by Prince Ahmed and accosted the Sultan of the Indies.

"You have asked for me. See, here I am. What would you have of me?"

The sultan said nothing but placed his hands before his eyes to avoid the sight of so terrible an object. At this rude reception Schaibar was provoked, after he had troubled to come so far, and he instantly lifted up his iron bar and killed the sultan before Prince Ahmed could intercede in his behalf. All that he could do was to prevent his killing the grand vizier, who had been sitting not far from the sultan and who now said to the prince that he had always given the sultan, his father, good advice.

"These are they, then," said Schaibar, "who gave him bad!"

As he pronounced these words he killed all the other viziers and flatterers of the sultan who were Prince Ahmed's enemies. Every time he struck he killed someone, and none escaped except those who saved themselves by flight.

When this terrible execution was over, Schaibar came out of the council hall into the center of the courtyard with the iron bar upon his shoulder. Looking hard at the grand vizier, who owed his life to Prince Ahmed, he said, "I know there is a certain magician here

113

who is a greater enemy of my brother-in-law's than all the rest. Let the magician be brought to me."

The grand vizier immediately sent for her, and as soon as she appeared, Schaibar said, at the same time that he swung at her with his iron bar, "This is the reward of your evil counsel!"

After that, he said, "This is not yet enough. I will treat the whole town in the same way if they do not immediately acknowledge Prince Ahmed, my brother-in-law, as their sultan and the Sultan of the Indies."

Then all who were present made the air echo with repeated acclamations of "Long life to Sultan Ahmed!" and immediately after he was proclaimed throughout the whole town. Schaibar ordered him to be clothed in the royal vestments, installed him on the throne, and after he had caused all to swear homage and fidelity to him, went and fetched his sister Peribanou, whom he brought with all the pomp and grandeur imaginable and made her the Sultana of the Indies.

As for Prince Ali and Princess Nouronnibar, as they had had no hand in the conspiracy against Prince Ahmed and had known nothing of it, Prince Ahmed assigned them a considerable province, with its capital, where they spent the rest of their lives.

Afterward Prince Ahmed sent an officer to Prince Houssain to acquaint him with the change and to offer him whichever province he liked best. But that prince thought himself so happy in his solitude that he answered with thanks for the kindness offered him, and said that the only favor he desired was permission to live undisturbed in his chosen retreat.

Sultan Ahmed and his Sultana Peribanou lived a long and happy life and brought to their people a wise and just rule.

Pearl S. Buck and Lyle Kenyon Engel

THE RIVER MONSTER

In the old days it was said that a monster lived in the rivers of Persia. Some of the elders claimed to have caught a glimpse of the monster on moonlit nights when he raised his head out of the waters.

Priests came to the banks of the river to make sacrifices to the monster, for it was believed that the monster had the power to cause terrible floods that ravaged the land.

The rain god, however, was very jealous that the monster had the reputation for causing floods because he actually caused them by sending great storms and torrents of rain.

So the rain god was angry with the river monster.

And the rain god came down to the river to duel with the monster.

The rain god came surrounded by fearful winds, rain, and hail. The river monster was afraid but battled bravely and succeeded in tearing out the eyes of the rain god. Since he could no longer see, the rain god gave up and went back to heaven.

Now the rain god was even more angry and jealous. He was afraid of being blind and tried to think of some way to get his eyes back. Finally he consulted a seer who told him he should descend to earth and marry a mortal who could help him get his eyes back from the river monster.

PERSIA

The rain god took the seer's advice and had himself led to earth to a small village. In his present condition the rain god was not the most appealing of bridegrooms but his wealth and position was sufficient for him to secure a bride.

Although the maiden he married was very poor, she was young and beautiful and worked very hard to be a good wife for the rain god.

After they had been married awhile he told her that she must help him get his eyes back. She was happy that she could do something to help her husband and looked forward to the day when he would be able to see.

The young bride went down to the river and sat on the banks awaiting an opportunity to try to seduce the river monster. It didn't take long because the river monster was so ugly no one had ever tried to seduce him before. He was overjoyed by the attentions of this beautiful young girl and was ready to give her anything she desired. When she finally asked him for the eyes of the rain god he got them for her without question.

As soon as she got the eyes, the young bride ran home to her husband with them. When the rain god had his eyes again he was overjoyed to see what a beautiful wife he had. And his bride was so happy that her husband could see she gave thanks to the gods every day.

But the rain god was not satisfied simply to have his eyes again. His heart desired to take revenge upon the river monster for his years of blindness. So once again he went off to do battle with the river monster.

This time the rain god succeeded in killing the river monster. And he returned home triumphantly to his wife with the head of the river monster.

But his wife was horrified when she saw the head of the river monster. She had not wanted to help with a murder. And in her shame and anger she went and threw herself into the river and died.

Tanya Lee

116

THAILAND

THE WATER FESTIVAL

Every year, on the 13th of April, the people of Thailand celebrated the Song Kran or Water Festival. Each person turns to his neighbor and pours a little water over his hands. This is done in commemoration of an old legend about an evil king with magic powers.

Long, long ago a very wicked king ruled over the land. He was so cruel and so powerful it was said that he was in league with the devil. When he went to war he would always win. If any spear hit him, it would simply bounce off leaving no wound. He was not content just to capture enemy soldiers but tortured them in the cruelest ways he could think of.

Everyone was afraid of the king. If a slave displeased him it could mean death. If a courtier disobeyed him, he would be exiled from the kingdom. And his twelve wives fulfilled his every wish without question.

All of the king's wives were beautiful but there was one—the youngest and loveliest of all—who was his favorite. This girl was also very clever. So clever, in fact, that the king never suspected she had a brain in her head. The more she thought about how horrible the king was, the more his favorite wife desired to find a way to free the people from his cruelty.

One night when they were dining together she praised him for his great power and endurance. "You are the most powerful man on earth," she told him. "You cannot be defeated in war. No one dares to disobey you. Everything is done exactly as you want it to be done. Does this mean you are a god and will rule as king fore-ever?"

"No, I am not immortal," the king laughed. "Every man must die someday. But I am lucky because there is only one way I can be killed. I can be strangled." By this time the king had drunk too much wine and was talking more freely than he should have.

"You are so powerful, it's not possible that anyone could stran-gle you," the lovely wife said. "There is no man on earth strong enough to do it."

"It will not take strength because that is my weak spot. That is the way I am destined to meet my end," the king said. "But let us talk no more of unpleasant matters."

They retired and when the king had fallen into a deep sleep, his wife took her long silk veil and wrapped it gently around the king's neck. Then she pulled it tight and his head fell off entirely. She picked it up and screamed in horror. The other wives heard and came running to her aid. The king's head was cursing her and she passed it in fear to another wife. As he cursed each one, she passed the bleeding head to the next wife. When the head had reached the twelfth wife it died and she put it down on the floor. Then each wife poured water over the hands of the others to wash off the blood of the evil king. And that is why to this day people pour wa-ter over each other's hands to celebrate Song Kran or Water Fes-tival.

Tanya Lee

THE TIGER AND THE COW

In the jungle there lived a fierce tiger whom all the animals feared. He would kill any animal he could find whether or not he needed the food. The animals were unable to defend themselves from the beast and decided to try and bargain with him in order to save themselves from total destruction. They offered to sacrifice one animal a week to the tiger if he would then leave the others alone. The tiger agreed to this plan because he was getting old and was tired of chasing the animals.

The first animal to be sacrificed was a young cow. He was very young and did not want to die before he had a chance to enjoy the pleasures of life, but he knew it was his duty to sacrifice himself for the safety of the other animals.

And so slowly but determinedly the calf set out for the tiger's abode. He became very sad and stopped at the edge of a ravine and desperately cried out, "What shall I do?"

Instead of an answer the young cow heard his own voice echoing back to him the words "What shall I do?" Hearing this echo suddenly gave the calf an idea of how he could trick the tiger and save his life, and so with hope stirring in his heart he set off once again to the tiger's abode.

When the calf arrived, the tiger was very angry at him for being late. But the calf apologized to the tiger and then proceeded to tell him why he had been delayed.

"I would have been here sooner," explained the calf, "but I left home with my mother and on our way here we met another tiger who attacked and killed my mother. I was able to hide and later escaped and came here."

"Another tiger has eaten my food!" the tiger shouted out when he heard this. "I must fight this beast. Show me where he is living."

And so the little cow led the mighty tiger to the edge of the ravine, and told the tiger that his rival lived on the opposite side. When the tiger learned this news he shouted out to the tiger on the other side "Come here." But of course the only answer he got was his own echo repeating the words "Come here." The tiger thought that his rival was shouting back at him which angered him even more, so he was determined to cross the ravine and fight his newly found enemy.

He then realized that the ravine was very wide and he asked the calf how the other tiger had gotten across it.

"He just jumped across," replied the calf. "It seemed very easy."

The tiger was determined that he could do what any other beast of his kind could do, so he leaped across the ravine, but instead of reaching the other side he plunged to his death on the rocks below.

The little cow then went back home and told the other animals what had happened. The animals all praised the cleverness of the little cow and rejoiced because they could now live out their days in peace and happiness.

Tanya Lee

TIBET

TWO FOOLISH FRIENDS

There were once two friends who lived together in a small cottage. They were both poor orphans and shared all of their few possessions with each other. One day as they were walking through the village they noticed a sign that offered a reward of three gold coins to anyone who could capture the tiger which was threatening the village.

The two men thought how wonderful it would be to have the gold coins so they immediately began to devise a plan to capture the tiger. They worked for days building an elaborate cage which was sure to trap the beast. When they were finished with their work they began to discuss how they would share the reward.

The first friend said, "The reward will be quite simple to divide— one coin for me, one for you and one for me."

"Oh no," said the second friend, "that would be unfair, you will get two coins and I will get only one."

"Have you not heard what I have said?" replied the first friend. "One is all each of us gets—one for me, one for you, and one for me."

But the second friend still did not agree and the two friends began to fight. A neighbor came along and asked them why they were fighting. They told him of their plan to capture the tiger and of the argument they had over how to divide the reward. The neighbor then asked them how they planned to capture the tiger. They showed him the cage they had built and explained how they planned to capture the beast. The neighbor agreed that the plan was a good one and that they might be able to capture the beast but he told them they must first settle the argument over the reward. He suggested that they go to the wisest judge in the land and let him decide for them how they should divide the coins.

And so, after receiving directions from their neighbor, the two men set off for the judge's house. The neighbor gave the men wrong directions and it took them three days to reach their destination.

When they reached the judge's house they told him of their argument and asked him how they should divide the reward. The judge was quite surprised to hear their story and told them they did not have to worry about how to divide the coins because they would never receive the reward. The tiger had already been captured. While the two men were making the journey their neighbor had used their trap to capture the tiger and gain the reward.

When the two men heard this story they felt very foolish. They had lost the reward because they had argued over the reward. They vowed never again to fight over money, especially over money they did not even have!

Tanya Lee

VIETNAM

DIEM AND SIEM

There once lived a young man and his beautiful young wife. They had a sweet little baby girl and their happiness was unbounded. But when the daughter was still very young the mother became ill and died. The widower was very sad and sent his daughter whose name was Diem to live with her grandmother.

After several years the widower remarried. His new wife was herself a widow with a young daughter named Siem. After the marriage Diem came once again to live in her father's house. Her new mother was an evil woman and hated her stepdaughter. She made Diem do all the housework while she and her daughter spent every day in leisure.

The father was a court messenger and was often not at home. When he would return home from his travels his wife would tell him awful lies about Diem, and the poor man was forced to punish his own sweet daughter. He did not suspect that his wife would lie because she was always careful to hide her wickedness in his presence.

Diem was made to dress in rags while her stepmother and sister wore beautiful silk and lace gowns, which Diem had to sew for them by hand.

The stepmother had a beautiful flower garden where she spent most of her days in idleness, looking at the flowers and thinking she was like a flower herself.

One day the stepmother went to visit some friends; before she left she told Diem to spend the day weeding the garden. Diem worked all day in the hot sun, pulling weeds from the garden, while her stepsister played or just sat resting in the shade.

Siem watched her sister Diem as she worked in the garden and saw that even though she was wearing rags and was all covered with dirt, she was still more beautiful than all the flowers. She became very jealous and decided she would have to get rid of Diem if she was ever to get a husband. She thought that no one would marry her if they saw her beautiful stepsister. So when the sun went down and Diem left her work to begin preparing dinner, Siem went into the garden and plucked up all her mother's beautiful flowers.

When the mother returned home, Siem took her into the garden and told her that Diem had plucked up all the flowers along with the weeds. The mother was outraged, and dragged poor innocent Diem into the garden, and told her that if all the flowers were not back into the earth by morning that she would be sent away into the wilderness and never allowed to return home again. The stepmother knew that she had given Diem an impossible task, because some of the flowers had been pulled from the ground so harshly that they were already dead.

Diem worked all night in the garden. In the hour before sunrise when all the birds began chirping their morning songs, Diem looked around her at all the dying flowers and realized the hopelessness of her task. She began to cry. Suddenly she looked up and saw her grandmother standing before her. The grandmother had magic powers which she used for only very special reasons. She came now because only magic could bring the flowers back to life and save her granddaughter from being thrown into the wilderness. The grandmother told Diem to shed her tears over the flowers. As soon as her tears touched the earth the flowers began to spring to life looking more lovely than ever.

The next morning when the stepmother and daughter went down into the garden they were astonished to see Diem sleeping among the blooming plants. They had expected never to see her again, but when they realized she had performed this wonderful task they were more jealous than ever.

Not long after this it came time for the great court festival. Diem was forbidden to go but instead had to spend much time helping to prepare for the grand event.

The day arrived and Diem was left home to work in the kitchen. She had wanted to go, and was very tired and sad because of her hard life. She sat down in front of the hearth and began to cry, wishing she had been sent into the wilderness rather than lead such an unhappy life.

Once again her grandmother appeared to her and told her she was sorry her magic had only brought Diem a harder life. She gave Diem a beautiful set of clothes and brought her to the festival.

At the festival the king asked Diem to dance. She was very happy until she saw that her stepmother and Siem were watching her. She was afraid they would punish her when she got home, so she left the king and ran home. As she was running away she lost one of her slippers. The king had fallen in love with Diem and he picked up her slipper and declared he would marry the woman who could wear it.

All the women of the kingdom tried on the slipper and of course Diem was the only one who could wear it. She and the king were soon married and life became happy for Diem.

But the stepmother and Siem were more jealous than ever, and their jealousy made them more wicked. They decided to kill Diem. One night when they were visiting at court they put poison in Diem's food. She died very suddenly.

When Diem's grandmother heard of her death she rushed to court to try to save her. Alas, it was too late to save poor Diem but the grandmother was able to transform her into a lovely nightingale.

A year passed and the king had not stopped grieving for his lovely bride. One day when he was out hunting he heard the beautiful song of the nightingale and was enchanted. When Diem saw her beloved husband she flew down and landed on his hand. The love between them was so strong that Diem was transformed back into her human form by its powers.

Diem told the king of the evil her stepmother and Siem had done to her. They were banished forever from the land. Diem and her husband lived out their days in peace and happiness.

Tanya Lee

THE TIGER STORY

Long ago when the world was new and animals and men spoke the same language, the tiger looked quite different. His skin was the color of bright shining gold, and was without stripes. Although he was very beautiful he was also a vicious hunter and was feared throughout the land.

One day a farmer who had been plowing his field at the edge of the jungle, left his water buffalo to drink at the stream while he himself slept in the shade. The day was very hot and he slept for a long time.

The tiger, who had been watching from the jungle, pounced before the water buffalo. Before the beast had a chance to react in fear the tiger spoke to him in a gentle reassuring voice, "Don't worry, poor helpless beast of burden, for I have not come to harm you, but only to ask you some questions. Why is that you who are so strong allow that man who is so small and weak to work you all day in the hot sun?"

"I know not why it is," replied the big stupid water buffalo. "I only know that he has a magic power he uses over me called wisdom."

So the tiger approached the man, and with the same soft voice he had used with the water buffalo he said, "Man, I have learned that you have a great power that allows you to rule over the animals. Can you tell me how you got this power that I too might attain it and not so often go hungry?"

Now the farmer was a sly creature and immediately figured out a way to trick the beast. He told the tiger he would gladly share his magic power, but that first there must be a great ceremony.

With many magic words the farmer began to tie a rope all around the body of the tiger. He then gathered dry grass and twigs and placed them in a circle around the tiger. The great golden animal was struck silent with wonder at this ritual. But when the man lit a match to the grass and the flames soared, the tiger realized he had been tricked. The flames burned away the ropes and the tiger escaped, but to this day his coat is the color of tarnished gold and long black stripes remain as the scars of where the rope encircled his body.

Tanya Lee

I. K. JUNNE is a young art historian and folklorist who is well known for his translation of Oriental classics into English and French. A native of Seoul, he was educated at Korea University and the Sorbonne in Paris. His first children's book, *Long, Broad and Sharpsight,* appeared in 1971. He lives in New York, where he works on the research staff of a major network.